Dragons of Tellusara

The Skylight Dance

CONNER DOYLE

PAGE PUBLISHING
Conneaut Lake, PA

First originally published by Page Publishing 2024

ISBN 979-8-89157-521-9 (pbk)
ISBN 979-8-89157-541-7 (digital)

Special thanks to my mom, Joy Doyle, for all her
inspiration and support in writing this book.

Chapter 1

ELIANORA'S BIRTHDAY WAS COMING SOON, and turning twelve was an important event for every dragon on Loopdy Island. She stayed awake late that night as the family fire slowly faded, and the night sky, full of twinkling stars, reminded her it was time for all dragons to be sleeping. She tried to sleep, but thoughts of the Skylight Dance kept her mind excited. She finally fell asleep and dreamed of the perfect dance that she and her friends would perform for the entire island.

The entire class of twenty twelve-year-old dragons would fly effortlessly through the loopdy loops. As she waited for her turn to fly, she watched the red dragon with black outline lead the way with his head held high, followed by an identical red dragon with silver glistening brilliantly as she smirked and followed swishing her tail from side to side. Next, the brown dragon with golden spots shining like stars quietly took off, keeping his head low. The next dragon to join the dance was orange with white stripes bouncing as she anxiously awaited her turn. She was short for a dragon but beautiful and full of energy. Finally, Elianora took to the sky with her purple-and-blue scales glistening in the starlight following her friends. As she looked down at the ground, she noticed a green dragon with teal waves standing on the ground looking up at them with a sad expression on his face.

Elianora abruptly awoke, wondering, *Who was that green dragon? Why is he sad?* Then she heard her mother shouting.

"Elianora, breakfast is ready." Verity tried to shout loud enough but not sound harsh to wake her sweet daughter. Eleven-year-old dragon girls can be over dramatic, and Verity didn't want their day to start on a bad note. She hurried around the house packing snacks and checking her wings in the mirror to make sure the scales were shiny, and the sun would glint off the blue scales and her teal outlines so they could be admired throughout the day. She was a busy mom of four. Her children were all so wonderful, each in their own way. Raising three teenage daughters was a full-time job all by itself. But Verity couldn't give up her gem shop. She loved both her jobs, and being busy made her happy.

Kizzie, her fourteen-year-old brown with teal daughter; Nonie, her eighteen-year-old blue with red daughter; Stepharus, her twenty-seven-year-old red with blue son; and Cormax, her magnificent husband with his beautiful red scales and brown paws, chatted as they enjoyed their breakfast. Elianora finally joined her family with a smile and a quiet good morning. She had so much on her mind.

As the family flew away to start their days, as most dragons do, Elianora stretched out her wings to do a quick check in the mirror to make sure all her purple-and-blue scales were clean and polished, and her teal patterns were easily spotted. She headed for school full of energy.

As Elianora landed near the schoolyard, she saw her friends— Theadosia and Sukkey—talking with Dranex, who was Theadosia's twin brother; and Anthony, who was her boyfriend. Elianora joined her friends just as the school bell rang. The entire class of twenty dragons gathered in their "classroom" of soft green grass and settled in to listen to their teacher. Elianora had trouble focusing on what her teacher, Ms. Emelina, was discussing.

"Loopdy is a mountainous island that is rich in gems and minerals," Ms. Emelina excitedly informed her students. She turned her pink scales toward her students as she looked up at the loopdy loops. Her red outline highlighted the beautiful color of her scales. "It is famous for the spiral loops of gem-laden rocks that we all enjoy flying through."

Dranex perked up and smirked as he looked around at the other dragons. They all knew he was the best flier. His eyes fell on the emerald-green-and-teal dragon in the back row, who recently moved to Loopdy Island. "Yeah, flying, right, Shatter-wing?" Dranex sarcastically snarked.

"My name is Davarius," Davarius calmly corrected Dranex. His wing had been broken and healed for several months, and the negative comments and attention was something Davarius wasn't going to get upset about anymore. But the comments always brought to his mind the vision of him flying recklessly over the volcano belching steam and smoke on Pyreton Island where he was born. After he crashed, he couldn't move. It took hours for his family, friends, and dragon rescuers to find him. He regretted his crazy risk, but that didn't help his wing heal well enough to let him fly. He had hoped that moving to a new island would be a fresh start. It seemed Dranex was going to make that a challenge.

Theadosia smirked as her brother arrogantly raised his head. Sukkey and Elianora exchanged a look that communicated their disapproval and disgust. Anthony sighed quietly as he looked down at the ground. His friend and girlfriend could be mean sometimes. He was uncomfortable with it, but he didn't know how to change it or what to say to them about his dislike of their cruel treatment of other dragons. He thought about speaking to Davarius, but it didn't seem like the right time.

Ms. Emelina cleared her throat to draw her students' attention back to the lesson she was focused on today. She would have to talk to Dranex again about being disrespectful and unkind to others. Maybe she should contact his parents again. That hadn't seemed to change his behavior before; it probably wouldn't help this time either. She continued the lesson with a smile.

"Loopdy Island and the chain of islands surrounding it are thought to be about five thousand years old. The rich soil that is created by the lava flow is perfect for the grasses, trees, and flowers that cover about 75 percent of the island. It is a wonderful place for gem mining and selling as well as trading the many fruits and plants that dragons love to enjoy. The islands that are not as fortunate to have such a lush forest and variety of fruits trade some of their resources for the stunning variety on Loopdy Island. It is a wonderful world for dragons to be able to thrive," she concluded.

After class, the dragons stretched and talked with one another as they walked the short distance to their next class with Mr. Kristone. He taught biology and explained the different and, sometimes unique, talents that dragons possessed. It was more interesting than history to most of the young dragons. As everyone walked along, Davarius trailed behind the others. Elianora told her friends she would meet them in a few minutes and joined Davarius on the path. As she approached him, she realized he was the dragon from her dream last night.

"Hi, I'm Elianora," she greeted him with a shy smile. "I'm sorry about Dranex. He just doesn't know how to be pleasant to other dragons. He's really not that bad when you get to know him."

"I'm used to being bullied by other male dragons. For some reason, my wing makes many of them uncomfortable. They don't see me. They just see my disability. I try not to take it personally, but sometimes it gets hard to handle." Davarius tried hard not to show how hurt his feelings were. He wanted to make friends and just be a normal dragon.

"So maybe after school we could share a fizzy juice and get to know each other a little better. My friend Sukkey, the orange dragon with white right up there, and I go to a special spot in the meadow to pick the best fruit and then make the fizzy juice with the bubbly water nearby. It's extremely delicious! What do you say?" Elianora tried not to sound too pushy.

"Sure, I'd like that," Davarius said calmly. "I haven't tasted fizzy juice before. It sounds awesome."

"Great!" Elianora said a little too loudly. "I'll see you after flight and physical education class."

Elianora walked forward to join Sukkey and the others. They had just gotten settled for biology class to begin. Davarius smiled and found a comfortable place in the back where no one would bump into his wing.

Mr. Kristone hushed the students. "Today we're going to talk about how dragons get their color. The simple answer is genetics. You get your color from the genes that are combined from your parents. Most dragons have a primary color with a secondary color that is a highlight of stripes, dots, or outlines. For instance, I have a primary color of green with purple highlights. Some dragons end up with two primary colors, but one of those colors is more dominant than the other. Rarely, dragons have three colors. Most often, these dragons have two primary colors, and one color that is a highlight." Mr. Kristone paused and pointed to Elianora. "For instance, Elianora has purple and sapphire blue as her primary colors and teal that outlines and dots her various features."

Elianora smiled as the students turned and looked at her. She knew it was rare to have three colors, and she really did love that she was unique, but she really didn't like to be the center of attention. She tried to just sit still.

"Your genes also determine if you are a male dragon or a female dragon. A male dragon has chromosomes from their parents that are an X and a Y, while females get an X from both parents so they have an X and an X. Of course, no one can tell what chromosomes you have by looking at you." Mr. Kristone tried to gauge the dragon's interest in what he was explaining. They didn't seem too bored, so he continued. "All of you have fifty chromosomes, and each chromosome has many genes. The genes for your color are on the forty-eighth chromosome."

The students giggled quietly and exchanged glances with one another. Color was something unique to each dragon, and they loved that. Telling the difference between male and female dragons was rather boring to them. The only reason to know the difference was when you wanted to have offspring. None of them were ready for offspring, no way.

Mr. Kristone taught for over forty-five minutes. Finally, he concluded the lesson and dismissed the young dragons. The dragons all stood and stretched as they walked away in groups. They were all friends, but they usually stayed in smaller friend groups when they were not in class. Davarius walked alone behind the groups of dragons. One more class, and school would be done for today. He was looking forward to going home and then going to have his first taste of fizzy juice.

After a fifteen-minute break, the dragons arrived at the last class, which was taught by Mr. Ferrix. He is an expert flier that taught them about physical activities like stretching, walking, and flying. The best part was flying. All the dragons look forward to flying. After all, it is what dragons do best. Without being able to fly, a dragon wouldn't be able to get between islands or gather some of the luscious fruit that was higher up on the mountains.

Elianora couldn't imagine not being able to fly. She suddenly realized that Davarius couldn't fly. *I wonder if his wing will ever be strong enough to fly again?* Elianora mused.

"What are you thinking about?" Sukkey asked as she bumped her friend playfully. "You look like you're far away."

"Oh, nothing," Elianora answered. She didn't want to talk about it right now. "By the way, I invited Davarius to go with us to the meadow after school and enjoy some fizzy juice."

"I…I uh…uh sure okay," Sukkey stammered. "I guess that sounds like fun."

"Don't tell the others," Elianora whispered. "I don't want them to come along and start making fun of his wing again."

"Right, no problem," Sukkey whispered back.

They sat in a comfortable place in the clearing and settled in to listen to their instructor, Mr. Ferrix, who was pacing back and forth in front of his students with his blue scales shining and his yellow outline glistening in the sunlight. This was the best class of the day, flying.

"All right everybody"—Mr. Ferrix began—"spread out so there is room for everyone to stretch. We always stretch for at least ten minutes before flying, right?" He prompted the students.

"Right," the group of students answered in unison. They always stretched in class before flying, but most of them were young enough that they didn't want to be bothered with stretching most of the time. They just took to the sky.

Davarius stayed to the side in the back. He didn't want anyone to accidentally bump into his wing. He couldn't stretch like everyone else. His wing was healed, but it just didn't work the way it used to work. He watched as the other dragons stretched their wings toward the sky and then spread them out as far as they could. He stretched his right wing in the same way, but the left wing only went part of the way up and over half of the way out. No one seemed to notice him, and he was glad.

"Okay, you're going to fly in pairs today. Up to the top of the peak, through the loopdy loops and then back around to the end of the line. Keep going until everyone has had at least three flights. Line up, let's go!" Mr. Ferrix instructed his students. He walked back to where Davarius was standing. "You're with me today," he said quietly so only Davarius could hear him. He signaled for Davarius to follow him a short distance from the other dragons. "I want you to work on stretching and strengthening that wing. The stronger it gets, the better you'll be able to use it."

"I'll do my best," Davarius quietly replied as he shrugged his wings. "It really doesn't work very well."

"I know. I heard about your crash and your injuries. But we're going to try to get that wing in the best shape possible, deal?" Mr. Ferrix encouraged his young student.

"Sure, deal," Davarius answered, trying to sound confident.

After more than an hour, all the dragons except Davarius had flown at least three flights, and Mr. Ferrix concluded the class with another stretching session and dismissed them for the day.

Elianora and Sukkey found Davarius in the back. "This is my friend Sukkey." Elianora introduced her friend to him.

"Hi, nice to meet you," Davarius politely answered as he looked over at Sukkey.

"We'll meet you in the meadow in about an hour. It's the one to the east and slightly south almost to the eastern shoreline. Do you know where that is?" Elianora finished politely.

"Sure, I've walked there often since we moved to Loopdy Island," Davarius answered, "see you in an hour."

The three dragons parted and headed to their homes. Elianora was excited about their meeting, and Sukkey just shook her head and giggled at her friend. Elianora always made friends with everyone. Sukkey admired that about her friend.

Chapter 2

ELIANORA LANDED IN THE MEADOW near Sukkey. "Hey, have you been waiting long?" Elianora asked Sukkey as her eyes darted around looking for Davarius.

"No, I just got here." Sukkey chuckled as she noticed Elianora's nervousness. "You're so funny," Sukkey teased her friend.

Elianora tilted her head to her right side and swished her tail. "I'm just looking forward to sharing a fizzy juice with a friend," she whispered, pretending she had no idea what Sukkey found so funny. She lifted her head as she heard a rustling in the leaves. Davarius was walking toward them. "I almost forgot he would be walking, not flying," Elianora whispered to Sukkey, feeling silly. Of course, he couldn't fly to the meadow. She shook her head and walked toward Davarius with Sukkey close behind her.

"Hi, I found the right place, I see," Davarius said cheerfully as he watched the two dragons gracefully walk toward him. He noticed that Sukkey was shorter than Elianora. "There are tons of fruits growing here. It's amazing!" he added, admiring all the gorgeous trees and flowers surrounding them.

Sukkey cleared her throat as she lightly bumped tails with Elianora. "They are beautiful. Which fruit would you like to try first?" she asked, trying to break the tension. She had never seen Elianora so quiet and unsure of herself.

"I recommend the kumquat and cherries," Elianora added, trying to focus on the fruits.

"Sounds great," Davarius said calmly. "I haven't really had either of those. On Pyreton Island, it's too hot to grow those fruits. We have coconuts and pineapple mostly."

"I'll pick the cherries," Elianora announced, "and, Sukkey, you pick the kumquats, okay?" she added, moving quickly toward the cherry trees.

"Sure, no problem," Sukkey cheerfully agreed as she found a basket to collect the kumquats.

Davarius watched as the friends collected the fruit and then followed them over to a table and benches. The fruit smelled wonderful, but he wondered how they were going to make a drink out of them. He didn't want to be rude, so he just watched quietly.

"Let's go get a pitcher and the fizzy water at the fountain," Elianora said, pointing in the direction of the fountain as she picked up the baskets of fruit and began walking in the right direction. "We can use the press to crush the fruit," she continued.

Davarius quickly caught up with Elianora while Sukkey walked a little behind them. He was strong and could walk rapidly. Elianora was impressed with his muscular body and his rather tall stature. She thought of him as weak because he couldn't fly. As he walked beside her, she could see she was wrong about that assumption. *Well, that's a pleasant surprise!* she thought as she gave him a smile.

They made their way to the cart holding the glasses and pitchers, and Elianora selected a beautiful purple glass pitcher with matching glasses. She set them on a tray. "Can you please carry the tray?" she asked Sukkey. "I'll juice the fruit," she added as she set down the baskets of fruit next to the press and set a bowl under the blocks of stone that they used to press together so the juice would run out of the small hole that was made in the bottom stone.

"Of course," Sukkey replied. She wondered how long Elianora was going to try to do everything herself. The thought made her giggle quietly to herself.

Elianora handed the bowl of fruit juice to Davarius and politely asked, "Would you mind carrying the juice?"

"No problem," Davarius answered, turning to follow Elianora and Sukkey to the fountain. "Wow, what an amazing fountain,"

Davarius commented in wonder. He had not seen such a beautifully carved fountain before. "I really need to explore the island more," he added. "Was this carved by someone you know?"

"Yes, it was. A local brown dragon made it by using his special magic," Elianora bragged as she filled the pitcher with fizzy water.

As Elianora carried the full pitcher toward the table, the bubbles made an effervescent, swishy sound, and the light sparkled off the bubbles that shot out of the pitcher and then gracefully landed back in the pitcher in the center of a bubbly swirl. Sukkey followed her carrying the tray of glasses. She looked at Davarius holding the bowl of fruit juice and told him pleasantly, "Thank you for carrying that back to the table."

"No problem," Davarius replied with a smile.

As the friends settled at the table, the girls began dividing the fruit juice into the glasses and used a bamboo straw to stir it together. Elianora poured the fizzy water over the fruit juice and offered both her friends a glass. She picked up her own glass and raised it in the air. "Welcome to Loopdy Island, Davarius," she announced, "here's to great friends and delicious fizzy juice."

"Cheers," Davarius added as he had his first taste of fizzy juice.

Elianora and Sukkey both smiled and chatted as they enjoyed the fizzy juice with their new friend. The three dragons spent over an hour sharing stories of Loopdy Island, school, and their favorite exploits. Sukkey told a few stories but mostly listened while Elianora told Davarius the names of the other young dragons at school. After finishing off the last of the fizzy juice, Davarius stood and placed his glass on the tray.

"Where do we put the dirty dishes?" he asked, looking from side to side.

"Oh, we'll take care of that," Elianora volunteered. "There's another tray over by the fountain to put the dirty dishes, so the dragon that lives nearby can clean them."

"I'll help," Davarius insisted. "I'm used to waiting on myself. It's part of the physical therapy routine I do to strengthen my wing, plus I'd like to help. Since I got hurt, I have become remarkably independent and self-sufficient," he added with a sparkling smile.

"Well, I have to get home," Sukkey interrupted. "I'll see you later," she added as she nodded to Elianora.

"Okay, I'll see you later," Elianora blankly answered her friend. Her mind was on Davarius. "Thank you for helping me," she said to Davarius as they walked side by side to the cart.

"You're welcome," Davarius said matter-of-factly.

They put away the tray and dishes and walked back through the meadow together. Elianora wanted to rush home to tell her sister Kizzie all about her day. She didn't want to be rude and just fly away, but she also didn't want to walk all the way home.

"Well, I need to get home," she explained politely. "My sister will be wondering about me."

"Yeah, me too," Davarius answered. "It's okay if you fly away," he assured Elianora as he noticed her hesitation. "Just because I have to walk, doesn't mean you do," he teased.

"Oh...oh, well okay," Elianora stammered hesitantly. "I'll see you tomorrow then," she added as she turned and flew away.

"She's really nice and kind too," Davarius said out loud to himself. He walked briskly back to his home. He couldn't wait to tell his mom all about his afternoon and his new friends, Elianora and Sukkey.

*****

Elianora landed in her front yard and rushed into her home. She looked around for Kizzie, but no one seemed to be home yet. As she turned, her brother, Stepharus, walked through the door.

"Hi," Stepharus said, smiling at his little sister, "what have you been up to today?"

Elianora paused for a moment, deciding whether she wanted to tell him about Davarius. After several minutes, she couldn't keep her excitement from spilling out. "I had the most wonderful afternoon. There's a new dragon in school named Davarius, and I spent the afternoon sharing fizzy juice with him and Sukkey," she divulged in a rush.

Stepharus was silent in shock. Finally, he sat down and asked her to sit with him so they could talk. "Is Davarius from Pyreton Island?" he asked.

"Well, yes, his family moved here not too long ago," Elianora answered hesitantly. "Why?"

"Well, did you wonder how he hurt his wing? Did he tell you what happened?" Stepharus said as he watched the questions sink into his sister's thoughts.

"He just said he was hurt in a flying accident, but not much more than that. How did you know he has a hurt wing?" Elianora was stunned by Stepharus's questions.

"Well, since he told you about his accident, I guess I can tell you. Remember a little while ago when I was called to Pyreton Island for an emergency?" Stepharus began. "Davarius crashed after flying too close to one of the volcanoes for too long. He was seriously injured. We had a hard time getting to him because of the smoke and heat. The air turbulence made flying to the location risky and extremely difficult. Finally, we had to climb on the ground, which took over an hour. He had a broken wing, but he was also delirious and couldn't move his legs. We thought he might have a broken back, so it took six of us to carry him down from the mountainside to a safe location. Once we got out of the smoke and steam from the volcano, we were able to fly him to the healer's den. They did surgery on him for over eight hours to repair his injuries. His back was bruised badly but not broken. His leg was badly sprained. His wing wasn't so lucky. They were able to put the bones back together, but he may never fly again. It was serious, Elianora. Truly it is a miracle he's alive." Stepharus looked curiously at Elianora. He normally didn't tell his family about the emergencies he worked on, but he didn't want her to be unaware of the seriousness of Davarius's injuries.

"So do you think he'll ever be able to fly again?" Elianora said quietly, trying not to cry. "That would be so awful for him. What if he cannot fly in the Skylight Dance?" she added, suddenly realizing her new friend might be excluded from the most important event in a dragonling's life. Turning twelve and celebrating the transition to dragonhood were what the Skylight Dance was all about. *How would Davarius celebrate his dragonhood if he couldn't fly?* she wondered.

"I don't know," Stepharus said quietly. "I'm sure he will be able to participate somehow. He just might not be able to fly."

"Wow!" Elianora was stunned. Her excitement about her afternoon faded away as she considered the possibility that Davarius might not be able to fly in the Skylight Dance. She shook her head as her thoughts raced. "Thank you for telling me," she replied. "I'll talk to you later," she added as she headed toward her room.

Elianora curled her tail around her as she laid down in the corner of her room. *How can I help Davarius?* she wondered. *There has to be some way to help him be part of the Skylight Dance.* Her thoughts raced as she puzzled over how to help Davarius enjoy the Skylight Dance as much as all the other dragons.

*****

Davarius walked briskly home. "Mom, are you home?" he called as he entered their home.

"Davarius?" his mom, Athien, answered. "Hi, you sound excited. What's going on?" she added.

"I just had the best afternoon ever." Davarius began. "I had fizzy juice with two of the girl dragons from school."

"Really?" Athien replied, smiling at his excitement.

"Their names are Sukkey and Elianora. They showed me the meadow on the east side of the island. It's beautiful. We had cherry and kumquat fizzy juice and talked. They told me stories about Loopdy Island and some of their crazy escapades. They didn't seem to care that I couldn't fly with them. They were really nice to me." Davarius finished with surprise.

Athien was smiling at him and patting his arm. "I'm glad you had a wonderful day with new friends. Tell me more about them."

"Elianora's tricolored," Davarius explained, "the most beautiful purple wings and scales with a royal blue underbelly and teal outlines. Just gorgeous! Sukkey is orange with a white outline stretching from her underbelly to her wings. Really gorgeous and unique!" He finished.

"They sound beautiful," his mom replied, "and like they could be really good friends."

"It would be nice to have friends like I did back on Pyreton Island," Davarius responded.

"How did the physical therapy go today?" Athien continued.

"I think I'm doing better," Davarius answered quietly. *I wish she wouldn't push me to try to fly when I'm perfectly fine walking,* he thought.

"I'm glad to hear it," Athien encouraged.

"I'm going to rest now," Davarius said as he headed toward his room. "See you at dinner."

Chapter 3

"HAVE A GREAT DAY!" VERITY shouted to her family as she flew off to work at her gem trading booth in the center of the island.

"I'm off to search out those rare treasures hidden up in the mountains today," Cormax informed his children. "Your mother and I won't be home until late tonight. You're all on your own for dinner. Be sure you get home by sundown," he added in his most somber fatherly voice.

Stepharus left early, and Nonie was gone too. Elianora and Kizzie swished their tails as they said their goodbyes and headed for school. Elianora was glad that Kizzie was in a different group of dragons from hers. She was a great sister, but she tended to be bossy when they were in the same classes at school. This was the second year that they had separate classes, and Elianora was happy that Kizzie was busy with her own friends instead of nosing into Elianora's business with her friends.

Elianora grabbed a piece of dragon fruit and a purple glass bottle of fresh, cold water as she sat outside her home and enjoyed the fresh morning air and the sounds of birds and animals as they all started their days. After finishing her breakfast, Elianora flew off toward school to meet up with her classmates.

She sat alone in the back of their first class. She had some thinking to do. *I wonder how I can get everyone to help me figure out how to include Davarius in the Skylight Dance since he won't be able to fly?* she pondered.

Sukkey sat down next to Elianora. "What are you doing all the way back here?" she teased. "I like to sit in the middle best because the teachers don't single you out for crazy questions to make sure you're paying attention," she added.

"I just thought I'd be different today," Elianora answered softly. "I was trying to figure out a way to get Theadosia, Dranex, Anthony, and you to help me make the Skylight Dance a little different this year so Davarius can participate," she boldly added.

"You want to do what?" Sukkey said in shock. "There's no way he can be part of the Skylight Dance—he can't fly."

"Really, I hadn't noticed!" Elianora snapped sarcastically.

The two friends sat in silence for a few minutes before they heard their teacher dismiss class. As the other dragons walked away, Elianora stood and turned to Sukkey.

"Sorry, I didn't mean to be snarky," Elianora apologized.

"Don't worry about it," Sukkey reassured her friend. "I should have known you would want to help Davarius. You always want to help everyone," she commented, smiling at her friend. "It's one of the things I like about you!" she added as they started walking toward the next class.

"Thanks, you're a great friend," Elianora said quietly. "Now any ideas about how to get the others to go along with a plan to include Davarius? Dranex doesn't like Davarius, and Anthony will go along with Dranex as usual. Theadosia always goes along with her twin brother."

As they got close to the group, Davarius came over to them. "Hey, how are you guys today?" he said cheerfully.

"Good," Elianora and Sukkey both answered at the same time.

They all laughed as they found a place to sit close to their other friends. Elianora wanted to have a plan before she tried to convince the others to help. She tried to pretend it was just another day, but she was determined to find a way to include everyone in the Skylight Dance and that included Davarius too. Luckily, no one noticed her distraction except Sukkey, of course.

As they arrived at their flying class, Elianora decided to keep an eye on Davarius while she was waiting her turn to fly. She wanted to see what he was able to do with his injured wing.

Maybe he could fly for a few minutes, she wondered. She enjoyed watching her classmates as they each soared through the loopdy loops. They all made it look easy, but she knew it wouldn't be easy for Davarius. It wouldn't be easy to convince twenty dragons to break with tradition and somehow include a dragon that couldn't fly. *It's unheard of,* she scolded herself silently.

When school was dismissed, the dragons all chatted for a few minutes and then each headed off in their own direction.

"So what's up with you today?" Sukkey asked, giving Elianora a sideways glance. "You've been quiet all day, so I know you're up to something. Give, what is it?"

"I'm just thinking about something I want to see happen at the Skylight Dance," Elianora answered, trying to sound excited.

There was an uncomfortable silence between the two friends as they walked toward home. Normally, they would fly away after making plans for later, but today, Elianora just wanted to be out in the meadow quietly considering how she could make this happen. There had never been a dragon that couldn't fly in the Skylight Dance. The finale included all the dragons flying in pairs and then ending with a group dance in the sky. It was always so spectacular to watch.

I can't ruin the dance for everyone else just to include Davarius. There's got to be a way. Elianora struggled to figure out some way to help Davarius and still stay with tradition and give the island dragons the amazing display the young dragons planned.

"I'll talk to you later." Sukkey finally broke the silence between herself and Elianora. "Whatever's bothering you, I'd be happy to help," she added, "if you'll let me."

"I just have to figure some things out," Elianora explained. "I promise I'll tell you soon. I'm sure I'll need your help."

"Okay, bye," Sukkey called over her shoulder as she flew into the air.

I have to think this through, Elianora thought as she flew toward home. When she arrived home, no one was there. She rushed into her room, pulled out a scroll, and started making notes. After an hour, she looked back at the last scroll and realized it looked more like scribbling than notes. The loopdy loop scribbles on the scroll traced the pattern of the dance they practiced every day for the last month. "There's no way Davarius can do loopdy loops with a wing that barely works, and it's so high up. There's no way to get up there without flying. This is impossible!" she shouted.

Elianora threw down her scrolls and bounded outside. She took off into the air heading for the meadow. She circled around once to see if there were dragons around and finally landed where no one seemed to be close. She walked over to the fountain and got a drink of sparkling water instead of her usual fizzy water. She sat in the shade of a tree and admired the mountains in the distance. As she stared at the side of the mountain with the loopdy loops the young dragons would fly through, she noticed a rock shelf a little more than halfway up the mountain. It was surrounded by trees and bushes with lush green leaves and purple and red flowers. *What if…* she thought.

She quickly put her glass away and flew up to the rock shelf, circling around to see what was around it up close. Finally, feeling safe enough to try to land on the rock shelf, she slowly made her descent. The rock was steady and large enough for one or two dragons to stand and look over the beautiful scene below. "This could work!" she shouted louder than she meant to shout. Elianora searched for a way off the rock that would lead down the side of the mountain.

The bushes were unusually thick, but finally she saw an opening. She carefully pulled back the leaves and found a path that seemed to lead somewhere. She looked side to side and finally stepped through the leaves. Her ears were perked up, and her senses were on high alert as she ventured forward. Carefully she made one step at a time through the bushes. As she poked her head through the last of the leaves she came into the sunlight and could see a path that led downward. It seemed to wind back and forth as it gradually dropped down the mountainside. After about half an hour, Elianora found herself near the bottom of the mountain. "I've never been there before," she said to herself.

"I guess flying above everything makes you miss some of the best views," Davarius said, smiling. "What are you doing walking down the mountainside?"

"Oh, uh, hi," Elianora stammered. "I'm just exploring the island. After walking with you the other day, I realized I hadn't seen some beautiful parts of Loopdy Island."

"You looked like you were investigating a mystery up on that rock cliff. I watched you land, and I wished I could fly up there. It looks beautiful from down here. How about up there?" Davarius added.

"Well, I just never noticed that rock cliff before. I've always been so focused on flying through the loopdy loops that I guess I never really looked at what I was flying over. I didn't want to lose focus and crash into the rocks that form the tight formation of the loopdy loops."

"Have you ever practiced your dragon focus?" Davarius asked.

"No, I've been so busy practicing the loopdy loops for the Skylight Dance I haven't spent much time on the dragon focus. Mr. Ferrix says we will perfect that skill next year, after the Skylight Dance is behind us." Elianora explained.

Davarius answered, "Well, since I don't have to work on flying through the loopdy loops, I spend some of my time sharpening my dragon focus."

"Can you sharpen your focus enough to find the path that leads up the mountainside to the rock cliff?" Elianora asked.

"No, not until I watched you walk all the way down the mountainside on that path. Before today, I didn't even know there was a path," Davarius answered.

"It's beautiful and not too difficult to climb. Of course, I was going down, not up." Elianora laughed. "You want to try going up with me? Can you, I mean, are you strong enough to walk all the way up to that rock cliff?" Elianora blushed as she tried not to sound judgmental.

"There's one way to find out." Davarius puffed out his chest as he started walking toward the path. "You coming?"

"Sure. But if we get too tired, we'll have to turn back," Elianora replied.

"Deal. If we, meaning I, get too tired, I'll let you know so we can turn back," Davarius said in a teasing tone.

"No, I didn't mean that." Elianora just shook her head and followed him as they started up the path. "How long has it been since you could fly?"

"Several months. The bones in my wing are mostly healed, but the membranes may never heal. I can't fly because the holes don't allow the air to lift my wing." Davarius explained.

"How did that happen?" Elianora tried not to sound too nosy. "I mean, I know about how you crashed, but how did the membrane get holes in it?"

Davarius paused and gave a long sigh. "I was flying over the volcano, and it was belching steam and smoke, which I thought would be cool to soar out of and show off for everyone. Unfortunately for me, the steam scalded through the membrane like a dried leaf hit by a spark. That's what made me lose my flight and crash."

"That must have hurt tremendously." Elianora tried to find a word to describe how she imagined it would feel.

"It did. Then I broke the bones when I crashed. I'm lucky I didn't break my neck or my back," Davarius said. "But I didn't, and I'm getting stronger all the time. I'm thankful to be able to have a life so I can help other dragons in the future."

"I admire your strength. It must have taken tons of courage and hard work to recover." Elianora encouraged him.

"I need a break. How about you?" Davarius tried to lighten the mood.

"Sure, I could use a break too. There's a couple of rocks we could sit on right over there." Elianora pointed just to the side of the path.

"Looks good to me," Davarius answered as he walked quickly toward the rocks.

Elianora followed him, wondering if he was tired. He didn't seem out of breath or even like he was walking slower. *I think he's just trying to be a gentleman for my benefit,* she thought as she sat down.

After a short rest, they started up the path again. It wasn't extremely steep, but it still took strength to keep going. They mostly walked in silence until they reached the grove of bushes that surrounded the rock cliff.

"I think this is it," Elianora announced as she began pushing aside leaves to make her way through them to the rock cliff.

Davarius helped hold back the leaves for her and then followed politely behind her. They stood side by side on the rock cliff looking out at the gorgeous countryside around them.

"Wow, this is magnificent!" Davarius exclaimed.

"It really is," Elianora added, smiling. "You don't seem tired at all."

"No, I'm not really," Davarius agreed. "I've gotten much stronger since I've been working to recover."

"So have you thought about the Skylight Dance?" Elianora remarked, trying to sound casual.

"No. I can't fly, and that's really what the entire dance is about, so I'll just watch like everyone else," Davarius said quietly.

"Yeah, I'm sorry you can't fly. But if there was a way you could be part of the dance without flying, would you want to?" Elianora asked.

Davarius thought for a few minutes and then answered, "I guess I would, but I don't know how that could happen."

"Can you glide?" Elianora proposed. "I mean with the holes and everything, can you?"

"I don't know. I haven't tried. The thought of flying terrifies me. I still have night terrors about my crash. I don't know if I could even try to glide." Davarius explained hesitantly, hoping she didn't think he was just a frail dragon not worthy of being her friend.

"Well, there's only one way to find out," Elianora announced confidently, "just give it a try."

Davarius looked at her with wide eyes, speechless.

"Not here!" Elianora added quickly. "I meant like down on the ground or something, like maybe try jumping off a small rock or something."

"Oh, good. You scared me there," Davarius said with a long sigh of relief.

The two dragons sat laughing on the rock cliff enjoying the beauty that surrounded them. It turned out to be a great day after all. They noticed a dragon flying toward them.

"That's my sister Nonie," Elianora explained. "She probably came to find me because it's getting late. I guess it's time to get going."

"Here you are," Nonie said in an irritated voice. "I've been looking for you for over fifteen minutes. You need to get home now."

"Nonie, this is my friend, Davarius," Elianora said in her polite, irritated voice. "I'll head home now."

"Nice to meet you," Nonie said as she started to fly away. "You better, or Stepharus will be upset."

"I hear you." Elianora rolled her eyes.

"I need to get home too," Davarius volunteered.

"I have time to walk with you," Elianora stated. "It's a lot shorter going down than it is going up."

"Sure, no problem." Davarius chuckled.

As they made their way down the path, they talked mostly about the gorgeous view and how much they were glad they discovered such a beautiful place. As they reached the meadow, they stopped.

"I'll see you tomorrow," Davarius said. "Remember, I don't mind if you fly."

"Right, I remember." Elianora laughed. "I'll see you tomorrow," she added as she took to the sky.

Davarius smiled as he walked briskly home. It had been a fantastic day!

Chapter 4

By the time Elianora made it home, Nonie had already explained to Stepharus where she found their sister. Her brother seemed a little annoyed but not angry.

"Sorry I'm late for dinner," Elianora apologized in her most quiet, contrite voice.

"Next time you're going to be late, leave a note or take a minute to send a message stone," Stepharus scolded his sister, trying to sound firm.

"I will, sorry," Elianora apologized again. "What's for dinner?"

"I made a new recipe with sautéed sweet potatoes and amaranth, along with a few other vegetables," Nonie explained. "I hope we all enjoy it."

"It's delicious as usual," Stepharus complimented Nonie.

After dinner, Elianora excused herself and went to her room. She wondered if Stepharus could give her some information about the membrane healing in Davarius's wing. *Maybe there's some way to put a leaf over the holes and temporarily give Davarius the ability to glide,* she thought. *Maybe having him glide from the shelf over the crowd of spectators could be the grand finale.*

Elianora drifted off to sleep and dreamed about the Skylight Dance.

*****

The next morning, she rushed out the door to school. She wanted to talk to Sukkey and share her ideas about Davarius gliding off the rock cliff. If she could convince Sukkey to go along with her, then they could come up with a plan to get Dranex, Anthony, and Theadosia to agree to the idea. If Elianora could convince those three, the rest of the class would be easy to convince.

"Sukkey"—Elianora started as she sat down next to her best friend—"I need to tell you about a plan I was thinking about for the Skylight Dance."

"I knew you would." Sukkey chuckled.

"Awesome, I need your help." Elianora added, "We'll talk about it after school."

"Sure, no problem," Sukkey said.

Elianora wasn't really paying much attention during class, except in flying class. She loved flying, and she certainly wanted to show off her flying skill so Mr. Ferrix would see she was serious about preparing for the Skylight Dance.

After school, Elianora asked Sukkey to follow her as she took off for the sky. She wanted Sukkey to see the rock cliff and understand what she was going to explain.

As they landed on the rock cliff, Elianora turned to Sukkey and smiled. "Beautiful, isn't it?" she started as she turned to look out over the scenery below.

"It's beautiful," Sukkey agreed. "How did you find it? I never realized this cliff was here before."

"Me either." Elianora continued. "I found it the other day when I was sitting under a tree in the meadow. I was looking at the mountain and thinking about the Skylight Dance and how Davarius couldn't be part of it because he couldn't fly. When I saw the cliff, I flew up here and found a path that goes from this cliff down the mountain. Davarius and I ran into each other, and we walked up the path so I could show him the cliff. He didn't have any problem getting up here. That made me start thinking."

"Of course," Sukkey chimed in, "you are always thinking about some way to help others. It's just in your DNA."

"So I was thinking that maybe," Elianora continued, completely ignoring Sukkey's comment, "Davarius could walk up to this rock cliff, and as the rest of us assemble in the sky after our final flight, he could glide over the crowd, and we could all fly down and join him as we all land one after another in the meadow. It would be spectacular, don't you think?"

Sukkey blinked and sat speechless for a few minutes. "Well, I guess it would look spectacular, but how are you going to convince Davarius to glide off a rock cliff? Or have you even mentioned this grand plan to him?"

"Well, not yet." Elianora began. "I wanted your help, and I wanted to tell you first to see what you think about my idea."

"Oh, and what plan do you have to convince all the other dragons to go along with this grand finale, especially Dranex and Theadosia?" Sukkey imagined their laughter as they refused to even consider changing the Skylight Dance. "We both know they don't like change, and if they won't consider it, no one else will either."

"I know. That's why I need your help to come up with a great plan to get them to agree," Elianora said, trying to sound hopeful.

"Right, like I'm so successful at getting them to listen, much less go along with anyone else's plan," Sukkey groaned as she tilted her head back and closed her eyes. *They'll never go along with this plan,* she thought.

"Okay, so I know it won't be easy, but I was thinking if I can get Davarius to agree, then I might have time to figure out how to convince them to go along with the plan. I'll have to play to their egos somehow." Elianora exhaled as she felt her excitement fade. "I can't do this alone, Sukkey. I really need your help!" she pleaded.

"I know, I know." Sukkey smiled as she conceded to helping her friend. "You know I can't ever leave you out on a limb."

"Thanks!" Elianora's excitement started to return.

"But first"—Sukkey paused—"you have to convince Davarius to go along with your plan. You're on your own with that one. I'll help you by going along, but you're going to have to sell him on the plan."

"Right, you're the best! First, I have to figure out how to make it physically possible to glide. That's going to take some research. I need to talk with Stepharus first. I think he will know how to make that possible. Then I'll talk to Davarius." Elianora smiled at Sukkey. "I better get home and get started!"

The two friends flew together from the rock cliff and waved goodbye to each other as they each headed home.

When Elianora landed at home, she was happy to see that no one was home yet. She waited outside, pacing back and forth and hoping Stepharus would come home soon. First, Kizzie, and then Nonie arrived home.

"Well, you're home," Nonie greeted Elianora. "I'm surprised. You seem to be gone every afternoon. What are you up to?"

"I'm not up to anything." Elianora feigned hurt, hoping that would make her statement more convincing.

"Yeah, sure," Kizzie chimed in. "We know that's not true. You're always up to something," she teased.

"Give her a break," Stepharus added as he walked up to the sisters. "She's just helping friends, as usual."

"Thanks," Elianora said. "Can I ask you some medical questions?" She knew that would get Nonie and Kizzie to leave quickly. Once they were alone, they sat down around the fire circle.

"So how can I help you?" Stepharus offered. Elianora always made him proud. He was pleased to help his little sister because he knew she was up to some grand plan to help someone. He was curious who she was helping this time.

"Well, you know about my new friend, Davarius." Elianora began. "I was talking to him about why he couldn't fly, and he said the bones were healed in his wing, but the membrane has holes that keep him from flying. Is there some way to mend those holes so he could maybe glide?" Elianora watched Stepharus as she waited for him to consider her request.

"Well, I don't know how you could patch holes in the membrane. You would need something that's light and flexible. Then you would need to figure out a way to cover the holes and somehow make that stay in place. As soon as the air current hits his wing, it would need to be strong enough to withstand the pressure of the current." Stepharus was thinking this through. "I'll tell you what"—he promised—"I'll talk to some of the healers and see if they have any ideas."

"That would be awesome!" Elianora exclaimed as she hugged Stepharus. "You're the best brother ever," she added as she hurried into the house heading for her room.

*****

The next day, Stepharus talked with multiple experts. They were able to repair membranes. They informed him there was a current patient that they were working with to try to do that very thing. Stepharus headed home to share his information with Elianora.

"Hey, I found out some information for you," Stepharus informed Elianora.

"Great, what did you find out?" Elianora asked impatiently.

"The healers said it is possible, and they have a patient they're working with right now. They didn't say who, but you might want to talk to Davarius before you poke around anymore. You may be trying to find answers to things he has already taken care of," Stepharus said as he tried to make Elianora understand that she can't just nose into other dragon's business. "I know you have good intentions, but it's not your business unless Davarius wants to share that information with you. While I'm not sure which patient the healers were referring to, I know Davarius has an injury that is rare. It might be him, but you need to be careful about prying into his private business."

Elianora said, "You're right. I hadn't really thought about this being something he didn't want my help with. I wasn't trying to pry. I was just trying to figure out a way for him to be part of the Skylight Dance."

"I believe you, Elianora," Stepharus reassured her. "I just think you should talk to Davarius and ask what he wants instead of deciding what he wants for him. I have to go to work. Think about what I said before you talk to Davarius. He might not want your help."

"I will," Elianora promised. *I should have realized the healers would already be working to help Davarius. I need to talk to him tomor-*

row and see if he really wants to be able to participate in the Skylight Dance.

*****

The next morning, Elianora walked past the mirror without even looking at her scales. She felt discouraged. She almost made a huge mistake. Hopefully, Davarius would want to take part in the Skylight Dance, even if he couldn't fly. She flew off toward school and hoped she would have the courage to ask the right questions and convince Davarius it would be worth the work.

"Hey, are you okay?" Sukkey asked as she realized Elianora seemed discouraged.

"Yeah, I'm fine," Elianora answered. "I just need to talk to Davarius about whether he really wants to be part of the Skylight Dance, and I don't know what I can say that will convince him to be part of it if he says no."

"Or maybe you should just accept his decision and be his friend. You always want to help, but sometimes dragons need to help themselves." Sukkey patted her friend's arm. "I know that's really hard for you, but I'm here if you need me."

"Thanks, you're the best friend ever." Elianora knew Sukkey and Stepharus were right. She just hoped Davarius would be willing to take part in the Skylight Dance, even if it was difficult.

School was the same as usual with Dranex and Theadosia always trying to be the center of attention. Elianora just wanted to get through with school and talk to Davarius. She looked around and wondered where Davarius was. She couldn't find him anywhere.

After school, Elianora headed home. She wanted to be alone. While she sat outside her house, a message stone landed in front of her. She activated the message stone and listened to the message. It was from Davarius.

> Can you meet me in the meadow? I could really use a friend to talk with right now. I'll be there all afternoon.

Davarius sounded serious.

Elianora left a note for her mom. She didn't know how long she would be gone. She wanted to be able to listen as long as Davarius needed her to listen. She flew off toward the meadow. As she landed, she searched for Davarius.

"Hi, thanks for coming," Davarius said as he walked up next to her.

"Sure, I'm happy to help," Elianora assured him. "Why don't we get some fizzy juice and find a place to sit?"

"Sounds good," Davarius agreed. "Cherry and kumquat sounds wonderful."

"I agree," Elianora smiled as they headed for a basket to collect the fruit and get the fizzy water. Once they were done, they found a quiet place to sit in the shade. "So what's going on?"

"I went to the healer today, and I'm not sure what I want to do with the information he gave me." Davarius started nervously. "So the bones in my wing are healed, but the membrane can't fill in the larger holes. They want to do a membrane patch on the two large holes. If it works, I might be able to fly again."

"That's great!" Elianora replied.

"Well, yes. But that means I might have to fly again." Davarius began to explain.

"I don't understand," Elianora responded.

"No one knows this, so you need to keep this a secret, deal?" Davarius insisted.

"Sure, I can do that," Elianora assured him.

"I'm not sure I have the courage to fly ever again. I used to be the best flier in my class. Then I crashed, and it was because I was so stupid. I thought I could fly over the volcano when it was belching smoke and steam. I should have known better. It was all my fault. How can I ever trust myself to fly and not make another ridiculous decision? I just don't know if I'm strong enough to take the risk. I don't know if I can trust myself again." Davarius paused, searching for a way to tell her how scared he was about flying. He just couldn't find the right words.

Elianora waited to make sure Davarius was finished. "I know I would be scared to fly again after a crash like yours. I can't imagine how much pain you've been through. And you're right, it will take courage to go through whatever procedure they need to do to fix the membrane but, most of all, to trust yourself to jump off the ground and fly again. I know you made a huge mistake by flying into the steam and smoke over that volcano. We all make mistakes, but we can only get stronger if we give ourselves forgiveness. I think it's easier to forgive someone else, but it takes courage to forgive yourself. That's the first step, I think. How about you, what do you think?"

"I think you're really brave and kind, Elianora. You're right that the first step is forgiving myself and learning to trust myself again. I'd really like you to help me. If you would help me." Davarius looked over at Elianora.

"It would be my honor to help you," Elianora promised. "Just tell me how I can help."

"Well, first, keep reminding me that I have to trust myself again. Then after my surgery, would you work with me and help me gain the strength to hop, flutter, hover, glide, and finally soar?" Davarius glanced up at the sky and took a deep breath. "If that is even possible."

"Okay. When is your surgery?" Elianora asked.

"I don't know yet. I just decided to have it done!" Davarius laughed. "See, you helped me already."

Elianora and Davarius sat and talked for a while, and then they headed home.

*****

The next day at school, Davarius found Elianora and told her his surgery would be tomorrow.

"Oh, wow, that was fast. I'll be waiting for you to come home. How long will you be at the healer's den?" Elianora asked.

"I'll just be there overnight. I can't start using my wing for a week. After that, I'll be able to start using my wing, but they don't want me to go too fast, or I could hurt my wing again. I'm not great at being patient, but I guess I'll have to learn," Davarius answered.

"Okay, well, I'll help you not to be in too much of a hurry to soar through the clouds again," Elianora teased.

Davarius laughed. He noticed Dranex and Theadosia glaring in his direction. He didn't care; he had bigger challenges ahead of him than gaining their approval.

The next day, Davarius had his surgery, and his mom flew toward the classrooms searching for Elianora to let her know everything went well. Elianora watched a green-and-yellow adult dragon land just in front of her.

"Hi, I'm Davarius's Mom, Athien, and you must be Elianora." She began. "I wanted to let you know that Davarius came through his surgery amazingly."

"I'm so glad," Elianora said to her. "Now the hard work begins."

"That's right," Athien answered. "I don't know how you convinced him to go through with the surgery, but thank you."

"I didn't convince him. I just told him he had to forgive himself and trust himself again. He did all the rest," Elianora replied.

"Well, thank you. He needs a good friend like you," Athien said as she walked away. "I'm sure we'll get to know each other soon."

Elianora smiled as she watched Athien fly away. *Tomorrow will be a busy day. I just hope I can help him stay strong and learn to trust himself again,* she thought.

"Who was that?" Sukkey asked as she walked up next to Elianora.

"That was Davarius's mom, Athien," Elianora answered. "He had surgery on his wing membrane today, and she wanted me to know he was doing well."

"Oh, well that's great. Did you figure out if he wants to be part of the Skylight Dance?" Sukkey whispered.

"Well, not yet, but since he had his wing repaired, I would guess the answer is yes. I'll see him tomorrow, and I'll ask him then." Elianora promised.

"Well, that's a good thing." Sukkey began. "Somehow Dranex and Theadosia found out about your idea to include Davarius in the Skylight Dance. They're not happy. Dranex doesn't want anyone to make changes because he's afraid someone else might be the star of the dance!" she added sarcastically.

"Great, just what I need, Dranex and Theadosia having a tantrum. They never change, do they?" Elianora added.

Chapter 5

Dranex; his best friend, Anthony; and his twin sister, Theadosia, walked slowly toward their classroom discussing the current lack of attention they were getting from Elianora. Dranex appeared to be in a less-than-happy mood, commenting as he snorted out some smoke. "The other day, I saw her hanging out with Davarius once again instead of with us. That was the fifth time."

Theadosia, ever the one to feed his ego, added, "Not to mention Elianora's plan to change the Skylight Dance all for a dragon with a broken wing."

Anthony piped up with meekness, "Maybe she's just trying to help a dragon out?"

Theadosia glared at her boyfriend. "Yet she is hanging out with him over us. Not to mention, she has yet to even introduce this Shatter-wing to us or even ask what we think about it," she said with a snide grin glancing at her brother.

Dranex remained silent, thinking, *What is she doing hanging with that Shatter-wing, not to mention laughing and having drinks with him and walking with him?* Dranex's mind was spinning, thinking about all the interactions he had seen between Elianora and Davarius. His jealousy was beginning to mount.

Theadosia stoked the very slow fire burning in Dranex. "Maybe she is not interested in you, or she is trying to create competition for you," she suggested with a quite smooth voice, ever keeping her deceptive grin.

Anthony retorted, "How would you even know that?"

Theadosia snapped at Anthony, whipping her scarlet-red tail, "Oh, Ant, you aren't a girl, are you? I am, and I happen to know about everyone!" She finished with a grin and hint of anger.

Anthony, ever the one to not anger or disagree with Theadosia, paused before answering her and chose to remain silent, giving up.

Dranex finally commented with a hint of doubt, "Do you really think so? She doesn't seem to be that kind of dragon."

Theadosia, putting her claws on Dranex's red scales, replied, "Of course, brother, what other option is there? She knows the original plan for you to take the final act and show your brilliant performance that you've been training for so long. She might have even figured out that you plan to amaze her and win her heart. But she wants to see if you're a tough dragon, brother."

Her words dug into Dranex's mind like an echo chamber of his jealous thoughts as he asked "Then what should I do? Should I confront her about this? I really want to impress her and make her love me," he added with a jovial yet concerned voice.

Theadosia smiled knowing that Dranex had taken the bait. "Let's talk to Elianora about it, and if we need to, we will have a chat with this Shatter-wing. I bet your strength and power, along with your shining red scales and intimidating black design, will scare your wimpy challenger off." Theadosia grinned, thinking, *This will teach Elianora what happens when she steps out of line.* The trio marched forward to talk with Elianora and Sukkey.

Sukkey noticed their approach and tapped Elianora on the shoulder. "Um, Elianora, the red twins are stomping in this direction with their brown nerd following close behind."

Elianora rolled her eyes and muttered under her breath, "Oh great! I haven't had time to prepare what I wanted to say to convince them to include Davarius."

"Time for your sales pitch," Sukkey commented, trying to encourage Elianora.

Anthony rushed forward to greet the two dragons with his brown scales and gold spots shimmering. "Hi, how are you guys today?"

Before Elianora and Sukkey had a chance to reply, Theadosia stormed up and snarled, "So where's your new boyfriend?"

"I don't have a boyfriend. Nor do I want a boyfriend," Elianora answered defensively.

Dranex retorted, "Then why have you been hanging out with Shatter-wing instead of us? We are friends, remember?"

"His name isn't Shatter-wing. It is Davarius," Elianora stated emphatically.

Sukkey stood quietly next to Elianora, thinking, *I'm not getting involved in this, but I can't desert Elianora.*

"Fine, whatever! Why are you hanging out with him all the time?" Theadosia answered, brushing aside Elianora's comment.

"He's new here, and I'm trying to make him feel welcome and be his friend," Elianora said calmly, taking a deep breath.

"Why?" Dranex retorted with an accusatory tone.

"What's up with you?" Elianora responded. "Why do you care who I'm friends with? I try to be friends with everyone," she added.

"Of course, you're the best friend to everybody, Eli!" Theadosia answered, belittling her. "We've been your friends for years, but you just ignore us and spend all your time with him. Then you want to change the Skylight Dance for everyone!" she shouted loudly.

Other students began to notice there was something going on, and they turned to watch.

"I just think that every twelve-year-old dragon should be included in the Skylight Dance, no matter what their problems are or how long they've been here," Elianora loudly proclaimed.

"So then what? Do all dragons need to change to let one dragon have the spotlight? Everyone knows Dranex is the best flier in this class! Now you want to change everyone's dance to accommodate a dragon who can't even be in the air for five seconds!" Theadosia argued confidently as she looked at the other students.

"I am the best flier. No one has successfully outraced me," Dranex proclaimed as he shoved Theadosia out of his way. "After all, I've been your friend for years. Now you want to hang out with this other dragon and pretend I don't matter." He finished with a huff and a puff of smoke.

"You're not acting like my friend right now, and I don't appreciate it," Elianora stated emphatically as Dranex stood looking at her, stunned.

Mr. Kristone rushed between Dranex and Elianora. "Enough, that is quite enough from all of you. Get to your class now!" he sternly ordered everyone.

Anthony gave Elianora and Sukkey an apologetic look as he took Theadosia's paw and helped her to her feet. "Let's go," he said to her and Dranex.

Dranex shrugged and followed behind Anthony and Theadosia, who gave him a glare as she turned away.

Sukkey and Elianora joined the other students and made their way to the next class. They found a quiet place in the back of the class.

"Are you all right?" Sukkey asked Elianora in a whisper.

"I think I'm all right. But I just messed everything up. They'll never agree to my idea, no matter what plan I can come up with to include Davarius," Elianora whispered back with sadness in her voice.

"We'll talk about it after school," Sukkey whispered quietly.

After school, Dranex and Anthony left quietly. Theadosia held her nose up in the air as the silver outline in her neck shimmered. She walked past Elianora and Sukkey in a huff.

Dranex paused to wait for Theadosia and sighed. *I want to say something,* he thought, *but what do I say?* He shook his head as he decided not to say anything, and the three of them walked away.

"Let's get some fizzy juice," Sukkey suggested.

"Sure, that sounds fine," Elianora agreed as they walked toward the meadow.

After getting their drinks, Sukkey and Elianora found a shady, private place to sit and enjoy their fizzy juice.

"I'm not sure I can wrap my head around what just happened at school today," Sukkey said quietly.

"I don't know either," Elianora answered. "Dranex was acting bizarre, don't you think?"

"It feels to me like they purposely started an argument with you," Sukkey added.

"I think so too," Elianora agreed. "Did I do something wrong? Did I ignore them? I wasn't trying to be mean to them. I was just trying to help Davarius, and they didn't like him, so I didn't include them. Just because I'm friends with them doesn't mean I can't be friends with anyone else. And just because I'm friends with other dragons doesn't mean they're not my friends too."

"Plus, you were planning on including them, but they didn't give you the chance," Sukkey encouraged her friend.

"As usual, Theadosia tried to cause trouble, and Dranex went along with her. He seemed angry and aggressive about Davarius. I don't know why. What has Davarius done to make them angry?" Elianora puzzled out loud.

"Of course, Theadosia is causing problems," Sukkey agreed. "She is an expert at making dragons feel bad or mad."

"It's how she controls dragons. I think Dranex got upset because Theadosia said something. Most likely she thinks just because I am being friends with Davarius means I don't want to be friends with Dranex," Elianora speculated.

"Enough about them. What do we do about Davarius and the Skylight Dance?" Sukkey asked.

"First, I need to talk to Davarius and ask if he wants to be included." Elianora began. "Then I could help him train to strengthen his wing. Then I need to talk to Mr. Ferrix and convince him of this great idea to include Davarius."

"What about Dranex and Theadosia? How are you going to get them to cooperate and go along with any changes?" Sukkey asked tentatively.

"Well, once Mr. Ferrix agrees, then I'll try to get them on board with the plan," Elianora explained.

"So how are you going to include Davarius in the Skylight Dance when he hasn't flown for quite a while?" Sukkey asked.

"Okay, here's what I was thinking," Elianora started to explain, "Davarius could be in the center of the formation as we're all standing in a row at the start. We do the dance just like we've practiced.

Then when Davarius is the only dragon left on the ground, he will take flight but stay fairly low to the ground. Then I was thinking Dranex and I will fly down to him, and then he will fly over to the rock cliff and land as Dranex and I start our pattern. We can help him get there if he can't do it alone. Then we start the landing like we practiced, and once every dragon is on the ground except Dranex, Davarius, and I, he flies from the rock cliff to join us and glides to his place in the line as we land in our places. That way, he gets to fly a tiny bit and be included in the dance. But it doesn't interfere with everything we've been practicing. It just adds to the dance."

"Wow, you really have thought this through. That plan could really work, not just for Davarius, but also for everyone else." Sukkey smiled as she realized Elianora had once again come up with a brilliant plan to include everyone and make sure not to change the plan drastically.

"We better get home before my mom sends my sisters to hunt me down again." Elianora laughed. "I'll talk to you tomorrow. Thanks for being such a good friend."

Chapter 6

Elianora woke to a sunny day. She could hear the birds singing as she got ready to find out how Davarius was doing. His mom told her he was coming home that day. Elianora wondered, *How long will it be before he can start using his wing? I'm sure the wing will take time to heal and strengthen.*

"Good morning," Verity greeted Elianora as she came to the firepit. "Since you don't have school today, what do you plan on doing with your day off?"

"I'm going to check on Davarius and see how his surgery went yesterday. What time do I need to be home for dinner?" Elianora asked.

"Be home by sundown. We're having a delicious dinner tonight," Verity responded with a smile as she watched Elianora fly away.

The air was crisp, and the songs of birds floated happily around Elianora as she flew to the eastern meadow. Davarius was supposed to meet her there for fizzy juice to tell her about his surgery. As she landed in the meadow, she noticed small dragonlings playing with their parents and smiled to herself as their laughter rang out and echoed through the meadow. Elianora enjoyed Loopdy Island. There was so much beauty all around the island to take in. The dragons were all pleasant, well, at least most of them. Of course, there were a few that liked to cause trouble, but she didn't let that ruin her day. Today started out so pleasantly, and she hoped it would be a happy day filled with good news for Davarius. She also hoped that he would want to participate in the Skylight Dance.

Davarius walked briskly toward Elianora and greeted her. "Good morning! It's good to be back on Loopdy Island and away from the healer's den."

Elianora turned toward Davarius with a smile. "How did your surgery go?"

Davarius walked toward a nearby bench and sat down as he answered, "Well, they were able to repair the holes in my wing with grafts. They'll always be a different color and look somewhat odd, but they should work." He opened his wing and showed her the holes that had been covered with leathery skin that were shed from a lyran. "Now I have to be patient and let them heal before I can start physical therapy again. I'm hoping that someday I'll be able to fly again."

Elianora took a seat on the bench next to Davarius and thought, *That really is unique. He'll always have the reminder of those holes."* She said out loud, "That's great! I hope you'll be able to fly someday too. How long do the healers think it will be before you can start physical therapy again?"

Davarius answered, "They say three to four weeks. I go back in three weeks for them to check my progress. The hardest part is going to be waiting and not being able to work on getting my wing stronger. My mom says I have to be patient, or I could undo all the healers' hard work to repair the wing. I'll wait until they say I can start working on physical therapy again, but I don't know how patient I will be about that wait," he added as he laughed.

Elianora laughed with her friend and then asked, "How about a fizzy juice?"

Davarius stood up and answered, "That sounds great! Let's try a different fruit this time. What other fruits are around here?"

Elianora stood and declared, "There are so many fruits on Loopdy Island. We have dragon fruit, lemons, limes, oranges, plums, peaches, and pineapple."

"Whoa, that's a long list," Davarius interrupted. "How about peaches? And you pick another fruit you haven't mentioned yet."

"Sure, that sounds great." Elianora laughed as she started walking toward the peach trees. "Can you get a basket and meet me over there please? I'll pick some peaches and then some blueberries."

"No problem," Davarius responded, "I'll grab the basket and follow you."

Elianora walked to the tree and picked a few peaches and then turned to find Davarius close behind her. "Here you go. I forget how fast you can walk," she added. "The blueberry bushes are just over this way," she said as she pointed in the direction she was walking.

"Right behind you," Davarius announced as he followed her. "How do I tell if these blueberries are ripe?"

"If they're blue and plump," Elianora announced, "then they're ripe. Just be gentle with them when you pick them, or your paws will be stained blue!" she added, chuckling.

After gathering their fruit, they walked silently over to the fizzy water fountain and crushed the fruit and mixed it with the fizzy water. Elianora handed Davarius two glasses, and she carried the pitcher of fizzy juice back to the bench.

"It sure smells delicious," she said as she began pouring the juice into the glasses. She set the pitcher on the ground between them and took her glass from Davarius.

Davarius took a sip and said, "It tastes fantastic! Fizzy juice is one of my favorite things on Loopdy Island. Pyreton Island doesn't have fresh fruit like we do here. Maybe all this awesome fruit will help me heal faster."

"I don't know if it will help you heal faster, but it will keep you happy while you're waiting for your wing to heal," Elianora encouraged.

As they sat enjoying their fizzy juice, Davarius explained more about his surgery. "I've had three surgeries on my wing so far. Hopefully, this will be the last one," he said.

"Hopefully, you'll heal wonderfully and get to fly again soon." Elianora began. "I was thinking of an idea for the Skylight Dance. Would you like to hear about it?"

"Sure, I don't think I'll be able to fly by the time the dance comes around. I'd love to be part of the dance, but I don't know if I'll heal enough by then," Davarius confessed.

Elianora looked at Davarius and patted him on the shoulder as she continued. "I'll help any way I can. I was thinking about that rock cliff we went to on the side of the mountain where the loopdy loops emerge from the top. I was thinking that you could glide down at the end of the dance and join the rest of us as we line up after the finale. Then I started thinking that maybe there would be some way you could fly up to the rock cliff. It's not nearly as high as the loopdy loops, and we could make it part of the dance. What do you think?"

Davarius sat silently for a few minutes, and then he answered slowly, "I don't know if I would be able to fly that high by then. It's only a few months away. Plus, I doubt the other dragons would want to change the Skylight Dance. They've been working on their performance for a long time. I don't want to mess things up for everyone else. You're so kind to try to include me. Thank you."

Elianora sat looking at Davarius before she replied, "You wouldn't mess anything up for the other dragons. It would only add to the performance. It would be spectacular and different from all the other Skylight Dances I've ever seen. That would make our Skylight Dance special. If your wing isn't strong enough to fly up to the rock cliff by the time of the dance, then at least you could glide down at the end. I really believe you could be strong enough to surprise everyone. I'm sure I can convince the other dragons to include you. Dranex and Theadosia will protest at first, but I know Dranex. In the end, he'll do the right thing. He's tough on the outside, but he really does have a kind heart when it counts. If I can convince him, then he will be able to win over Theadosia. I didn't want to say anything to any of them until I talked to you. What do you say?"

Davarius tilted his head to one side and said, "I would love to be part of the dance. I just don't know if it's possible, but it would give me a goal to reach and give me incentive to work hard. If you can convince all the other dragons, I'll work hard and do my best not to disappoint them. Besides, it would be fun to see all the dragons watching the dance when they realize I can fly!"

Elianora clapped her paws together and tried to contain her excitement. "Yes, this is awesome. You'll be able to do it. I'll help if I can. This is going to be spectacular! Oh, I can't wait. I think we should talk to Mr. Ferrix first. He'll be the one that helps you with your physical therapy, right?"

"You're right," Davarius answered. "I think we need to talk to him first. He's in charge of the Skylight Dance, right?"

"Yes," Elianora confirmed, "he's in charge of the Skylight Dance. He's easygoing and smart. I'm sure he'll agree to help us figure this out and get everyone on board."

"That sounds like a great plan." Davarius began. "I have to get home now. I promised my mom I wouldn't be too long. She worries about me when I have surgery. We'll talk more about this later, Elianora," Davarius stood and looked into her eyes, "thank you. You are such a good friend. Thank you for including me. I'll do my best not to let you down."

Elianora stood and smiled. "You're welcome, Davarius. I'm sure everything will work out, and the dragons on this island will be so surprised when they see what we have in store at this year's Skylight Dance. We'll talk again soon. Take care of yourself."

Davarius and Elianora put away their glasses and pitcher and walked together in silence toward their homes. Finally, Elianora broke the silence. "I'm going to fly from here. See you later," she said, as she leapt into the sky and flew away.

Davarius watched her fly away for a few seconds before he started walking again. He was excited to have such a nice friend and to think about the possibility of being able to be part of the Skylight Dance. He couldn't wait to get home and tell his mom all about Elianora's plan.

*****

Elianora flew over to Sukkey's house and found her outside reading. "Hi, how are you today?" Elianora greeted her friend.

Sukkey looked up from her book with a smile and replied, "I'm doing wonderful today. How about you? I thought you were meeting Davarius this morning."

Elianora sat next to Sukkey and started to explain. "I did meet Davarius this morning. We shared some fizzy juice, and I explained my plan for the Skylight Dance to him. He agreed!"

"That's great," Sukkey replied. "Now you can remind me about this grand plan."

Elianora laughed as she realized some of the details of her plan had changed slightly since she explained them to Sukkey. She repeated her idea about the rock cliff and Davarius gliding to join the other dragons at the end of the dance. "Then," she added, "if he gets strong enough to fly up to the rock cliff, I was thinking he could fly up to it when Dranex and I fly up to start our dance. It would be a huge surprise to everyone to see him able to fly, even if it is just a short distance. We might need to help him, but if not, then we would just go on to do our dance in the sky with the other dragons."

"Wow"—Sukkey began—"that would be wonderful. How do you plan on getting all the other dragons to go along with this change of plans?"

"Well"—Elianora started—"first, we're gonna talk to Mr. Ferrix and see if he'll allow the change. I think he will, and then I'll explain it to Dranex and convince him to go along with the plan. I'll tell everyone else and hope they will want to include Davarius in the most important event in a twelve-year-old dragon's life. Surely, they won't deny that opportunity to Davarius. Dranex and Anthony will have to help us convince Theadosia. Will you help me?"

Sukkey smiled at Elianora. "You're my best friend. Of course, I'll help you."

Elianora hugged Sukkey, and they sat and talked for about an hour about the plan, the dance, and other things best friends talk about. "Would you like to fly up to the rock cliff and check it out with me?" Elianora asked.

"Sure," Sukkey replied, "I need to tell my mom where I'm going. Be right back."

Elianora and Sukkey soon flew off to explore the rock cliff. The sun shone brightly, and the light breeze carried the scent of flowers. As they landed on the rock cliff, they heard someone talking quietly on the other side of the bushes.

"I'm not sure." Someone was saying. "I just know I saw her and Davarius walking up this path one day. I thought maybe if we walked up here, we could figure out what they were up to."

"That's Dranex," Elianora whispered, "and Theadosia."

"And probably Anthony," Sukkey whispered back.

They stood near the bushes silently listening to Dranex, Anthony, and Theadosia. Suddenly they heard Theadosia complain. "I don't see any reason they would be climbing up this path. The path doesn't lead anywhere. It just stops a few feet up from here."

"There's just a bunch of bushes going up the mountain." Anthony added, "Maybe they were just exploring and didn't really have any particular reason for walking up here."

"Yeah, maybe you're right. I just don't understand why Elianora insists on hanging out with Davarius," Dranex grumbled. "Let's go find some shade in the meadow. They like to hang out there too. Maybe we'll run into them there."

"You know Elianora makes friends with everyone. She just likes all dragons and is always the one to include all of us, especially when a new dragon joins the island," Anthony explained.

Dranex glared at him and moaned, "Yeah, yeah, I know."

Elianora looked at Sukkey and shook her head. They stood close to the bushes so they wouldn't be seen when the trio flew away.

Theadosia whined, "I know you want to be the star of the dance. Don't worry, you and Elianora are the last dragons in the sky at the end of the dance. You'll be a shining star! Can we get off this mountain now?"

Dranex shook his head. "Let's go. You don't know how the dance will turn out," he said as he flew up into the sky.

Theadosia turned to Anthony and said, "I know it will be the most spectacular Skylight Dance that has ever been seen on Loopdy Island." They flew up to join Dranex.

The three of them flew away and down toward the meadow. Elianora and Sukkey stepped into the bushes to be sure they weren't seen.

Elianora waited a few minutes and then stomped out of the bushes. "Do you believe the nerve of Dranex? He wants to be the star of the dance like the rest of us aren't as special as he is!" she shouted.

Sukkey quietly answered, "No. I'm not surprised though. He thinks he's the most spectacular dragon on this island and can say and do whatever he wants. He's going to be really mad when you tell him you want to include Davarius at the end of the dance."

"This is going to complicate my plan for the Skylight Dance," Elianora complained. "I was so excited, and now I find out Dranex is going to ruin everything trying to be a show-off!"

Sukkey encouraged Elianora calmly, "It'll be okay. We just need to come up with a way to get him to go along with your plan to include Davarius. Surely, Dranex won't object to including Davarius because he'll be certain everyone will be paying attention to him the entire time. He'll be showing off as usual."

Elianora sighed. "You're probably right."

Sukkey walked around the rock cliff checking out the view. "You're right. It's not too far from this cliff to where we'll all be landing and forming our final line to end the dance."

Elianora took a deep breath and tried to focus on her plans for the dance. "Exactly," she replied, "and Davarius could glide down and join the line just as the last of us are landing. It would be amazing."

Sukkey smiled and suggested, "I'm sure it will be spectacular. Now why don't we go to the beach and relax for a while?"

Elianora looked surprised and responded, "That's a great idea. Let's do it."

They flew off together toward the beach on the west side of the island to be sure they were away from the east side, where Dranex, Theadosia, and Anthony went.

As Elianora dug her claws into the cool sand, she said, "The ocean is so beautiful. We haven't come here in a long time. We need to do this more often."

"I agree. I really like this side of the island. It's a great place to watch the sunset." Sukkey finished.

The two dragons sat on the beach in some shade for a while and then decided to go for a walk along the water's edge.

Elianora said, "It's been an eventful day. It went a little differently from what I had expected, but it was still a good day."

Sukkey suggested, "There's some shade over there under those trees. Let's sit there and watch the sunset before we head home."

Elianora agreed and then realized she told her mom she would be home by sundown. "I have to send my mom a quick message. She said to be home by sundown. I'll have to leave as soon as the sun sets."

Sukkey responded, "I better send my mom a message too, so she doesn't worry."

The two friends sat in the sand and sent their message stones. They talked quietly as they watched the sunset.

"That was gorgeous," Sukkey exclaimed.

"It really was beautiful," Elianora responded. "I better get going."

"Yeah, me too," Sukkey agreed. "Let's go."

The two dragons flew off together toward their homes and waved farewell to each other as they parted ways. Elianora was glad to be home. She wanted to enjoy dinner with her family and then get a good night's sleep.

Chapter 7

THE NEXT THREE WEEKS SEEMED to crawl by. Ms. Emelina spent time in her class going over the history of the Skylight Dance.

Ms. Emelina explained, "About a hundred years ago, Tellusara was ruled by a tyrant. There was danger everywhere around the mainland called Dracanosia. The adult dragons decided to send their children that were twelve years old or younger to safety somewhere far away from the tyrant king. The children prepared to leave and flew together into the dark sky to find refuge. After flying for many days with only short breaks, they were all very tired and lost. They looked up into the night skies and saw a glow of colorful lights. They decided to follow the lights that seemed to move across the sky. As they followed the lights, they were led to the chain of islands that they named Sanctuary Islands. That is the chain of islands that we live in today. To commemorate their journey, the council of dragons, who were part of the group of young dragons that came to Sanctuary Islands, developed the Skylight Dance to celebrate the blessing of a new home. From then on, all twelve-year-old dragons performed the Skylight Dance to remember how the young dragons were saved by the colorful lights in the sky and to mark the beginning of becoming an adult dragon."

Anthony raised his paw and asked, "Why did the young dragons stay on the islands and never try to find their way back to their home?"

Ms. Emelina answered with a heavy sigh, "The young dragons were lost, and the colorful lights disappeared and have never returned to help guide them back home. As they grew up, they loved the islands and decided to stay. Many dragons have tried to find Dracanosia. However, none have succeeded so far."

Elianora was humming as she and Sukkey walked together to their next class. She was nervous but excited. This would be the beginning of putting a plan in motion for Davarius to strengthen his wing and be ready for the Skylight Dance. The healers had cleared him to start physical therapy, and he was ready to get started. The last three weeks seemed to drag by slowly, but they were finally done.

"Good morning," Elianora and Sukkey greeted Davarius as they walked close to him.

"Hi," Davarius said as he smiled and waved at them, "I'm excited to get this wing strong. Thanks for helping me get through the last three weeks. It seemed like they were never going to end."

"You're welcome," Elianora replied. "I'm glad I could help. Now the real work starts. Let's go talk to Mr. Ferrix before class starts."

"I'm ready," Sukkey interjected. "I don't know how I can help, but I'm happy to help."

The three of them walked over to Mr. Ferrix, who was standing away from the class looking over his notes. "Good morning," he greeted them cheerfully. "How is everyone this morning?"

Davarius quickly answered, "We're all doing great. We have something to ask you," as he glanced toward Elianora and Sukkey.

Elianora cleared her throat and quietly explained, "Davarius has been cleared by his healers to start physical therapy again. I was thinking of a way that we could include him in the Skylight Dance. He has six weeks to strengthen his wing with your help." She took a deep breath and continued, "I was thinking that would be enough time for him to be able to glide and maybe fly a short distance. There's a rock cliff on the side of the mountain near the field where we'll be doing the Skylight Dance that has a path going up to it." She pointed toward the cliff hoping none of the other dragons noticed. "I was hoping Davarius could fly up to it and then glide down and land in the line during the finale when the last two dragons land also. If he can't fly up, then he would have time to walk up the path and be ready on the rock cliff to glide down. Just in case he doesn't have time to get strong enough to fly by the time the Skylight Dance is performed."

Davarius added quietly, hoping he wasn't overheard, "I think I will be strong enough to fly up to the rock cliff. It's not so high, and my wing is feeling great."

Sukkey chimed in, "Besides, if we all help him do his exercises, it should work."

Mr. Ferrix replied with a smile, "Well, that is an ambitious plan. I think it would be wonderful for Davarius to be included in the Skylight Dance, along with everyone else in the class. I'll help you get ready, but I have the final say on if you're strong enough to make the flight up to the cliff, deal?"

Davarius smiled and quickly agreed, "Deal. Thank you so much!"

Elianora gave Sukkey and Davarius a high five and knuckle punch. "This is great. Now all we have to do is convince everyone in the class to go along with the change of plans for the Skylight Dance," she said nervously.

Sukkey encouraged her friend, "You can convince them. I'm sure they'll be happy to include Davarius in the dance."

Mr. Ferrix said, "Let's get class started."

They all took their places, and Mr. Ferrix began by saying "We have six weeks left to practice the Skylight Dance. We'll spend all our class time working on the dance from now on. Since it is tradition to include every twelve-year-old dragon in the Skylight Dance, we will be making a few slight changes to be sure that Davarius can take part just like everyone else. I'm still working on the exact details, so for now, we're going to go over to the field near the mountain where the Skylight Dance will be performed and work on the dance as we've been rehearsing. Once I have it worked out, I'll fill you all in on the slight changes."

Dranex and Theadosia looked at each other and then turned and looked at Davarius, Sukkey, and Elianora.

Dranex whispered to Elianora, "This is all your doing, isn't it?"

Elianora smiled and answered, "I had something to do with it, but it's not all my doing."

Mr. Ferrix clapped his paws and instructed, "Okay, class, let's head out to the field and line up in order and stretch before you start the practice flight. First, I want everyone to fly up and around. Then after three flights, I want you all to practice going through the loopdy loops five times. After that, we'll start practicing the lineup. Let's get going!"

Mr. Ferrix pointed at Davarius, Elianora, and Sukkey. "You three, follow me."

They followed Mr. Ferrix and noticed Dranex and Theadosia whispering together with Anthony as they started to leave.

Dranex whispered, "I knew she was up to something. I don't think it's right to change everyone's Skylight Dance just for one dragon. Do you guys think that's fair?"

Anthony spoke up. "I don't think it's a big deal. After all, the Skylight Dance always includes every twelve-year-old dragon. It's tradition."

Theadosia glared at Anthony and said, "Not a big deal? Why should we all have to change everything just for one dragon? Dranex is right. It's not fair."

Mr. Ferrix called out to the class, "Enough chatting. Let's get in the line and get busy practicing." He turned to Davarius and said, "I want you to start by doing gentle stretches for at least five minutes." He moved away from Davarius and motioned for Elianora and Sukkey to follow him. "As I figured, Dranex and Theadosia are whispering together. Knowing you two, I figure you have a grand plan that will help convince Theadosia and Dranex to go along with the changes. Everyone else seemed happy to let Davarius be part of the dance. You two get busy practicing and scheming." He chuckled.

Sukkey and Elianora looked at each other and sighed.

Elianora said, "Of course they would be the ones to resist changes. We'll talk to them. Thanks for your help, Mr. Ferrix."

"You're welcome," Mr. Ferrix answered. "I'll let you know if any other students object. I don't think it's going to be a problem. You'll have to fill me in on the details of your plan later," he added with another chuckle.

"Sure, after class if that works," Elianora responded.

Mr. Ferrix nodded his head and walked back to Davarius to help him begin his physical therapy.

Elianora and Sukkey flew over to the field and headed for the line to begin taking their turn practicing flying. At the end of class, Dranex walked over to Elianora with Theadosia and Anthony standing a short distance away.

Dranex asked Elianora, "Why do you think all of us should go along with changing our Skylight Dance just to include a dragon who can't fly?"

Elianora answered, "By the time the Skylight Dance comes, Davarius may be able to fly, at least a short distance. Besides, he will at least be able to glide by then. It's tradition to include all twelve-year-old dragons in the Skylight Dance."

Dranex said, "It's not fair for all of us to have to change our plans for the Skylight Dance just because Davarius can't fly. Besides, he's new here. Why doesn't he go do a Skylight Dance on Pyreton Island?"

Elianora replied quietly, "He doesn't live on Pyreton Island anymore. He lives on Loopdy Island, and he should be included in the Skylight Dance with his class. That's not unfair. That's tradition. Besides, I know you wouldn't want to be left out if you were the one that couldn't fly."

Dranex stared off in the distance, thinking for several minutes. Finally, he looked at Elianora and said, "Well, you're right. I wouldn't want to be left out. I guess it wouldn't be fair to exclude Davarius either. I just want the Skylight Dance to be the way we have planned it. How do you plan on including him without changing everything?"

Elianora explained, "The dance will be pretty much the same. The only differences would be that Davarius would be in the middle of the line, and when everyone has taken off, he would fly up to the rock cliff up there." She continued as she pointed up to the cliff. "He would wait on the cliff while we do our routine, and then when the last two dragons begin to land, he would glide from the cliff, and all three of us would land in our places at the same time. It's not a huge change, just a little change to include Davarius along with the rest of us."

Dranex tilted his head to one side and thought for a few moments. "Okay, it sounds like it wouldn't be too much of an interruption for the rest of us. And it would follow tradition. That is important." he said thoughtfully. "I'll have to convince Theadosia to go along with it. You'll have to give me a few days, but I agree with you it wouldn't be right not to include all twelve-year-old dragons."

Elianora smiled and replied, "Thank you, Dranex. You're a good dragon and a good friend."

Dranex smiled and said as he walked away, "You're welcome, friend." He joined Theadosia and Anthony, and the three of them walked away.

Sukkey patted Elianora on the shoulder. "Nice job, friend," she announced.

After class, Elianora and Sukkey joined Davarius and Mr. Ferrix while all the other dragons left.

"I talked to Dranex," Elianora said, "and he said he would go along with the plan. He said he would talk to Theadosia and let me know. I'm sure if they both go along with the new plan, then Anthony will also."

"That's great," Davarius responded.

"I knew you could convince him," Mr. Ferrix added. "He's really a good-hearted dragon when he's with the right dragon. He just needs a little convincing every now and then. I'm sure he'll be able to convince Theadosia. She usually goes along with her twin brother. And you're right, if they agree, Anthony will most likely agree, if he doesn't already."

Elianora smiled and began to explain her plan. "So my plan includes putting Davarius in the middle of the line. When the last two dragons, that's Dranex and me, fly up, Davarius would fly up to the rock cliff. If he can't fly, then he would walk up the path on the mountain and appear on the rock cliff. That would just take a little longer. He would watch the dance and do some moves on the cliff while all the others are doing the dance we've rehearsed. Then when everyone finishes their part of the dance and begins to land, two by two, Davarius will wait until Dranex and I start our descent, since we're the last two dragons to land. When we get just past the cliff, he will glide between us, and all three of us will land together in our places."

Mr. Ferrix thought for a moment and then replied, "That sounds great. You have it figured out whether Davarius can make the flight or not. We just need to work on some cool moves for him to do on the cliff instead of in the air and then practice several times so everyone knows what to do. I like it! I really think if you work hard," he said looking at Davarius, "you'll be ready to fly up to that cliff and surprise everyone."

Davarius stood tall and announced, "I know I can do it. I just have to work hard. I never believed I would ever be able to fly again, but I'm starting to think it's possible. Thank you, Elianora, for giving me hope again. You really are a good friend."

Elianora shrugged her shoulders and answered, "You're so welcome. I'll help you any way I can. I have faith you can do it."

Sukkey laughed and said, "I agree! I'm happy to help too. And you're right. Elianora is the best friend ever."

As school ended, Anthony found a shade tree to read his new book. Dranex flew above him and landed next to him.

Dranex asked, "What book are you reading?" He walked over and sat next to Anthony.

Anthony looked up at Dranex, surprised. "Oh, I'm reading about the young dragons that found Sanctuary Islands."

Dranex replied, "Sounds like an interesting read and something you would like. I need to talk to you about this Skylight Dance stuff."

Anthony closed his book while saying "Okay, what's going on?"

Dranex began to explain. "So I talked to Elianora about the changes, and I think she makes a good point that it's tradition to include all twelve-year-old dragons in the Skylight Dance. The changes are not very big, and they would let Davarius be included in the Skylight Dance. Plus, the changes wouldn't really affect us or my master plan. What do you think?"

Anthony said encouragingly, "I agree with you. I think it's only fair and right for all twelve-year-old dragons to be included, and that includes Davarius."

Dranex smiled and said, "Great, now you can unite with me to convince Theadosia to go along with the plan."

Anthony added, "You somewhat egged her on to resist going along with these changes. But I'll do my best to help you change her mind."

Dranex jumped up with excitement and said, "Thank you. How about we talk to her tomorrow morning before school?"

Anthony nodded and answered, "Sounds great. Now if you don't mind, I'm going to go back to reading my book."

Dranex chuckled and said, "See you later, nerd," as he flew away.

Chapter 8

Dranex woke up to the morning sun shining through the window. He stretched thinking. *Now…I just need to meet up with Anthony, and then we can convince my sister to agree with the Skylight Dance changes Elianora came up with.*

As he got ready for school and executing his plan, he heard a fancy yet strong voice coming from below. "Dranex, Theadosia, breakfast is ready!" his dad, Callamdon, called.

Dranex flew down the stairs excited for breakfast, making a rather spectacular landing. "Good morning, Dad and Mom," he said as he entered the main dining room. His mom, Greta, was eating her breakfast and reading the news scrolls, not paying much attention or mind to Dranex. Meanwhile, Callamdon was busy making a hearty meal as he cut the fish and spewed hot flame to cook the fish in a matter of minutes. The fire made his red scales glow and the gray dots on his wings sparkle. Dranex sat down near the table and watched Theadosia walk down the stairs with her head held low. She had an annoyed look of someone who woke up on the wrong side of the bed. Dranex, being snarky, asked, "How are you, sleepyhead?" as he looked at Theadosia.

Theadosia irritably responded, "Just fine, bonehead!"

Callamdon put breakfast on the table and said, "Now, now you two, you've got a big day of school ahead. After all, you have the Skylight Dance you two have been practicing all month, right, sweetie?" He finished looking at Greta.

Greta put the news scroll down and walked to her gem case to choose one of her many necklaces made of different gems and colors.

She wanted to match her beautiful orange scales that were stunningly outlined by black. She always liked displaying her gems for all visitors so they could see her proud jewelry-making skills.

Greta replied, "Yes, we are very proud of you both for all the hard work you have done. One day, I'm sure you will do good work for yourselves." She walked over to her husband and kissed him on the cheek as she said, "Now I have important business. I will see you both at sundown. I expect good work from both of you." She walked outside and took flight to go to work as she always did in the morning.

Callamdon looked at them as he ate his breakfast. "So, Dranex, how is it going with your girl Elianora?" he teased.

Dranex happily replied, "Great, Dad. My plan will work. I just know it. The Skylight Dance will be perfect for me to ask her to be my girlfriend, and it will be the most amazing day of my life."

Theadosia interjected, "It would if it weren't for that stupid new dragon showing up. Mr. Ferrix has changed the entire thing just for this new dragon."

Dranex responded, "Maybe, the changes won't be so extreme. They won't affect everyone, maybe just Davarius." Theadosia gave a stink-eye look at Dranex, puzzled at what he just said.

Callamdon laughed. "I am sure Mr. Ferrix has a good reason for making the changes. Who is this Davarius?"

Theadosia started a rage-filled rant. "He is an off-island dragon from Pyreton Island. He even has a busted-up wing because he was an idiot. And then Elianora decides to change everything for this stupid d—"

Callamdon shouted at her sternly, "Theadosia! We do not talk badly of any dragon, especially ones that have such injuries, no matter what the reason."

Theadosia shut her snout as Dranex worried how he was ever gonna get his sister to agree to the changes. Callamdon went back to his calm, gentleman's demeanor. "Well, it is time for you two to get ready and go to school, my little comet and ruby." He kissed both of them on their heads as he helped them get ready for school and watched them start their flight to the school.

Theadosia glared at Dranex.

Dranex gave a look and said, "What? You were the one who was insulting Davarius in front of Dad."

Theadosia responded in confusion, "What is going on with you? I thought you hated the change of plans just as much as I did?"

Dranex decided he could at least start the war to convince Theadosia. He said, "I don't hate it as much as you do. I only disliked it at first because I wasn't told what the plan was that Elianora made. I thought they were going to change everything."

Theadosia replied in a passive-aggressive tone, "You know the plan now then?"

Dranex proudly replied, "Why, yes, I do, and it won't ruin any of my grand plan to make Elianora my girlfriend."

Theadosia responded demandingly, "Well, then what exactly is her grand plan?"

As they flew toward school, Dranex explained Elianora's plan to Theadosia. Theadosia didn't seem to be giving any ground to Dranex. They finally arrived and saw Anthony waiting patiently at the entrance.

Theadosia, noticing Anthony waiting as per usual for her, snarled in a very annoyed tone, "Hello, Anthony, did you know of Elianora's grand plan?"

Anthony stuttered and responded, "N-n-no, I didn't. What is it?" Dranex gave Anthony a worried look.

Theadosia ranted, "She plans with Mr. Ferrix to try and get this Shatter-wing to fly."

Dranex interrupted with an annoyed voice, "Davarius."

Theadosia rolled her eyes and went back to her rant. "He will try and fly with us. A dragon who can't even fly properly, even if his wing was healed, will embarrass all of us in front of all the dragons watching!"

Anthony responded, "How do you know he is gonna embarrass everyone?"

Theadosia snapped at him, "Oh please, we all know if a dragon breaks a wing, they can never fly again, especially in about six weeks' time. It's better for everyone if we just exclude him from the Skylight Dance and let him watch us work."

Dranex, tired of her attitude, angrily responded, "How would you like to be excluded then?"

Theadosia turned, gave a snarl, and said, "What?"

Dranex answered, "There was a time not so long ago when we were the outcasts and were excluded from things because we are twins!"

Theadosia stopped for a minute in silence, thinking back to when they were bullied and how they first met Elianora. Dranex quietly watched her and began to think back also. They both thought back to when they were six years old.

*****

They were new kids in the school after they moved to this side of the island with their parents. A dragon with black scales and a yellow underbelly cornered Theadosia and Dranex with his friends standing guard. The twins stayed next to each other as the bully dragon mocked, "Look, they are twins—the weirdos who look almost exactly the same—and they cuddled together to protect themselves. Look at 'em!" He and his friends began to laugh and make fun of Theadosia and Dranex.

Theadosia piped up, "We aren't weird! We're just different from you." She paused as she was thinking up an insult. Finally, she taunted, "Yellow belly jerk!"

The bully dragon, now angry at the insult, shoved Theadosia to the ground as Dranex pressed himself against the corner. The bully laughed and said, "Look, her brother is too scared, and the other one is too weak!"

They all laughed at them until a young yet strong voice rang out. "Hey! Leave them alone!"

Dranex looked up and saw a dragon with scales of beautiful purple, blue, and teal. "We don't bully anyone, especially dragons that are new and different!" the voice continued.

The bully responded, "You're one to talk, Elianora. You have three colors! You're about as weird as them."

Another young dragon with orange-and-white scales standing with Elianora said, "Leave them alone already. You had your fun, now leave."

The bullies laughed it off and said, "Okay, then see ya later, weird triplet squad!" They continued laughing as they walked away back to class.

Elianora turned around and looked at the twins and asked, "You both all right? He didn't hurt you, did he?"

Theadosia got back up after some assistance from the orange dragon.

Dranex also got up after lying in the corner. He looked at Elianora with her beautiful eyes and scales, truly a guardian angel to admire. Dranex responded, "Thank you. How can I repay you for such kindness, uh—"

Elianora responded, "My name is Elianora, and you don't need to repay me anything, though I would like to get to know you two if you want."

Theadosia smiled at the two and said, "Well, thank you for helping me and my brother."

The orange dragon also added, "And my name is Sukkey."

Dranex for the first time, much to Theadosia's shock, introduced himself. "My name is Dranex, and this is my sister, Theadosia, and I would love to hang out with you and have us get to know each other."

Elianora, with an excited voice, squeaked, "That sounds great!" The four dragons walked away together, and that was the start of them becoming friends.

*****

Dranex broke the silence and said, "We were both excluded and bullied because we were twins, but Elianora and Sukkey became our friends and even helped us stop getting bullied. Then we were accepted and made friends with the other kids in our class. What makes Elianora so great is she becomes friends with everyone and helps everyone no matter what. That is why I am going to ask her to be my girlfriend, because I love her. If agreeing to the changes helps her and makes it more likely she will accept, then I will happily go along with it. What about you, sister?"

Theadosia paused for a minute after listening to his speech. After thinking, she gave in begrudgingly. "Fine, you can tell Elianora I won't cause any trouble or fuss about the changes. But I still think this won't end well for anyone." She walked away quietly.

Dranex raised his claws in the air. "Yes! I finally convinced my sister to agree to something!"

Anthony looked at Dranex and gave him a high claw. "Good job, I am impressed. You managed to convince her. You didn't even need my help at all!" Dranex and Anthony chuckled as they walked into class.

Mr. Kristone greeted the class. "Good morning. I know you all are excited about the upcoming Skylight Dance. Since that marks the beginning of adulthood, I thought I'd talk about some of the abilities you will be learning about next year. I will only get into the basics and save the fascinating details for next year. As you know, as every dragon becomes an adult, they begin to get their powers. Some of these powers are dragon focus, fire breath, and various magical abilities."

He paused and waited for any questions. The young dragons sat quietly, anticipating what Mr. Kristone was about to explain. After a few seconds of silence, Mr. Kristone decided to continue. "Dragon focus is essentially being able to see and sense what is going on in the environment around you. For instance, you might be able to sense that a rabbit is close without being able to see it with your eyes. You might be able to focus your sight and hearing so you can hear or see more clearly. An example of using dragon focus is a blind dragon who can still fly and land safely. Mastering dragon focus takes years and is challenging to master."

All the students were looking around at one another, and *cool* seemed to be the word Mr. Kristone heard around the class.

Sukkey raised her paw and asked, "How will we know we can use dragon focus?"

Mr. Kristone answered, "It will be a gradual, subtle process. You will notice you can sense things around you that you didn't notice before. You will be able to hear a greater distance away. It will take concentration and practice to learn to use dragon focus."

Elianora turned to Sukkey and said, "That's awesome."

Sukkey replied, "That's how he always knows when we're talking instead of paying attention."

Mr. Kristone smiled and said, "That's correct Sukkey. Dragon focus does indeed allow me to know when you are not paying attention as well as hearing your comments."

The class seemed to laugh in unison.

Mr. Kristone raised his arms to quiet the class down. "Now on to fire breath. Dragons are born with a fire organ that allows them to breathe flame and store it temporarily. That organ does not develop fully until a dragon begins to mature into adulthood. At first, you will notice that you're able to spew little embers of fire. As you practice, you can use fire breath in different ways. Obviously, you can breathe fire out of your mouth directly toward an object. Eventually you will learn to control your fire breath to create a concentrated blast of flame. It takes practice to perfect the aim of that concentrated blast. It has a very explosive result, and we use it for many things. One example would be to mine gems from the terra. Your ability to breathe fire or create the fire blast will improve as you get older and build your stamina."

Dranex raised his paw and asked, "Are dragons resistant to that fire from other dragons?"

Mr. Kristone replied, "Dragons can be affected by fire breath. With the right force and abilities, a dragon can cause great harm to other dragons with it. We'll get into that complicated subject in the years to come. Magical abilities can be combined with dragon focus and fire breath. Different dragons have different magical abilities. The colors a dragon has determine what magical abilities they will have as they become adults. Your primary color means you will have a complete set of abilities connected to that color. Your secondary color means you will have only some of the abilities connected to that color. Those dragons that have three colors have abilities based on all three of their colors. Tricolored dragons are extremely powerful because they have all the abilities from both of their primary colors, plus several of the abilities from their third subcolor."

Elianora raised her paw and asked, "How can we find out what abilities are possible with the colors we have?"

Mr. Kristone chuckled and said, "For the rest of your school years, you will learn what powers relate to different colors and how to use those powers. This is one of the most complicated things that dragons must learn. You will probably be learning new things about your powers your entire life. Class time is over now, class dismissed."

As the dragons walked away, Dranex found Elianora. "I talked to Theadosia, and she reluctantly agreed to go along with the changes to the Skylight Dance."

Elianora was surprised. She was speechless for a minute and finally answered, "Well, that's great. I'll let Davarius and Mr. Ferrix know that everyone is willing to make the changes to the Skylight Dance. Thank you for talking to Theadosia and getting her to go along with the changes. I'm sure it wasn't easy. I really appreciate your help."

Dranex smiled and said, "No problem. See ya later."

Elianora looked toward Davarius as Dranex walked away. She thought, *What a relief! I thought that would be more of a struggle. Hopefully, there won't be any surprises later.*

Chapter 9

ELIANORA WAS ANXIOUS TO GET to school. There were only six weeks minus one day left to get Davarius ready for the Skylight Dance. As she flew through the blue sky, she looked down at the beauty below her. The brilliant colors of the island blended into a mural. The rich green leaves and orange, red, yellow, and blue fruits all mingled together to form the beauty of Loopdy Island. Seeing the beauty around her made her feel hopeful. As she landed at school, she noticed only a few students had gotten there before her. Sukkey wasn't there yet. Even Dranex, Anthony, and Theadosia hadn't arrived. As she landed, she spotted Davarius talking with Mr. Ferrix. She waved to them as she walked quickly toward them.

Mr. Ferrix cheerfully said, "Good morning, Elianora. You're here early also."

Elianora smiled and replied, "Good morning, Mr. Ferrix."

Davarius chimed in, "Good morning, Elianora."

After a few minutes of silence, Mr. Ferrix said, "I've been thinking about a plan to strengthen your wing, Davarius. Every day, even days when we don't have school, I want you to do five minutes of the warm-up exercise I showed you the other day. Once your wing is warmed up, I want you to stretch the wing out as far as you can without hurting yourself and then pull it back to your back as tightly as possible. The stretching needs to happen for at least ten minutes but no more than fifteen minutes. After that, I want you to relax. Repeat this process three times a day with at least three hours in between exercises. Make sure you're getting plenty of rest and sleeping comfortably at night so you have the strength to get your wing stronger."

Davarius was focused on Mr. Ferrix's instructions. He finally asked, "Why do I have to wait three hours to repeat it? And why only three times a day? Wouldn't I get stronger faster if I did it every hour and five or six times a day?"

Mr. Ferrix sighed and shook his head. "If you push yourself too hard, you will end up slowing your progress. Your wing hasn't been used for a long time, and you need to strengthen it gradually. Three times a day with at least three hours in between is pushing the limit. If you feel like your wing is getting too tired, you need to quit for that day. Trust me, you'll make more progress if you are consistent. I know you're anxious to get your wing strong so you can fly in the Skylight Dance, but if you overuse the wing, you will end up delaying the process, and you may not be ready for the dance. If you are able to do these exercises three times a day and you feel you can do more after one week, we'll talk about doing them more often during the day."

Davarius looked over to Elianora and asked her, "Will you help me keep track of the time when you're around? I know I'm going to want to push it too soon, and I need someone to hold me accountable so I don't mess this up."

Elianora smiled and said, "Of course, I would be happy to keep you on schedule. What are you going to do when I'm not around?"

"I'm going to ask my mom to help me," Davarius responded. "If I'm alone, I'll have to keep my mind on other things and be careful not to push myself too hard."

Mr. Ferrix patted Davarius on the shoulder. "You are strong. I'm sure you'll do just fine. Once your wing gets strong enough, then we'll try some hop flights and go from there. Now there's no time like the present to get started. Show me the warm-up and stretches."

Davarius moved back away from everyone and replied, "No problem." He began to warm up. The five minutes seemed to drag by.

Elianora watched quietly as Davarius finished his warm up and stretching. It took him fifteen minutes. She checked the clock on the wall and noted when three hours would arrive. She wanted to be sure to remind him if he forgot. Although she didn't think that would be necessary.

As school went by at a snail's pace, or so it seemed, the three hours finally passed. Davarius moved away from the other dragons, who were leaving as school finished for the day, and did his routine. By the time he had done the warm-up and stretching, he seemed tired. Elianora whispered to him, "Are you okay? You seem really exhausted. Maybe that's enough for today."

Davarius said, "I am tired, but I have almost three hours to rest. I'll be able to do the last series before I go to sleep tonight. It's just harder than I thought it would be. My wing is extremely weak."

Elianora felt concern for Davarius. "I'm sure you can do this. But give yourself a break. Slow and steady wins the race, right?"

Davarius chuckled. "Right, slow and steady will win the dance in this case."

Elianora laughed. "I've got to get home. Have a great night. I'll see you at school tomorrow." She finished as she flew away.

Davarius waved as he watched her fly away. He walked quickly home. He felt defeated. This was going to be harder than he thought. He thought, *I hope I don't let Elianora down or the other dragons who agreed to change everything for me.*

Elianora talked to her sisters, Nonie and Kizzie, about the plan for strengthening Davarius's wing and the progress he needed to make. "The idea is to have him strong enough to be included in the Skylight Dance, which is only six weeks away. He's really determined to get his wing strong enough to be part of the dance. I hope it doesn't take longer than the time we have. His wing is weak, and he seemed tired after doing his exercises twice. I'm just trying to stay positive so I can encourage him."

Nonie replied, "You will stay positive. You're always positive! Besides, Davarius seems very determined from the way you explained it, and this was just his first day. I'm sure it will get easier as days go by."

Elianora agreed. "I'm sure it will get easier. It's just hard to watch him work so hard and be so worn-out. But you're right. He is determined, and he doesn't need me or anyone else to bum him out and make him think he can't make it before the dance."

Kizzie chimed in, "I can't even imagine Elianora bumming anyone out." She paused and smiled to herself. "You are the opposite of a bummer. You're the most encouraging, hopeful, and inspiring dragon I know. As your sister, I can tell you I'm proud of you for that, even if it can be a little annoying at times."

Elianora giggled and replied, "Thank you, Kizzie. I needed to hear that. You're a great sister. I'll see you guys tomorrow. I'm going to go to bed now."

"Good night," Nonie and Kizzie responded in unison. "See you tomorrow."

Elianora hugged her mom and dad good night and even hugged Nonie and Kizzie before going to her room. As she settled in to sleep, she felt exhausted, and she felt like she shouldn't be because she hadn't done anything too exhausting really. It was going to be a long six weeks.

The rest of the week, Davarius worked hard on strengthening his wing. Every day seemed to blend into the other. Elianora and the other dragons in their class practiced the Skylight Dance every day at school in Mr. Ferrix's class. Davarius would watch them after completing his exercises, wondering if he'd ever be strong enough to be part of the dance. Mr. Ferrix kept encouraging him each day. Of course, the other dragons pretty much ignored him except for Sukkey and Elianora, who always made sure to encourage him before they left school.

When school was over, Davarius began walking toward his home. Elianora and Sukkey flew over him and landed not too far in front of him.

Elianora greeted him, "Hey, how did it go today? Do you feel like your wing is getting a little stronger yet?"

Davarius stopped to talk with them. "Maybe a little stronger. I don't get as tired by the end of the day as I did at first. Mr. Ferrix says I'm not strong enough to increase the number of times I can exercise. I'm afraid it's going to take too long, and I won't be ready for the Skylight Dance."

Sukkey replied, "Of course, you will. You're making progress, even if it seems slow."

Davarius shrugged his shoulders and said, "Yeah, I guess so."

Elianora reassuringly said, "You're doing great. Just keep doing those exercises, and you'll make it. I know it's frustrating, but don't let that stop you. You still have five weeks to get there."

Davarius smiled at both of them and responded, "Thanks you, guys. I am frustrated because I just don't want to let everybody down. All twenty dragons in that class agreed to change the Skylight Dance to include me. That's amazing, and I don't want them to be disappointed that they had the consideration to include me. I wouldn't just be letting my friends and myself down. I'd be letting the entire class down."

Elianora spoke softly, saying, "I understand how you feel. No one is going to be upset if you can't fly in the Skylight Dance. You're going to be included no matter what because you're our friend, and you're turning twelve just like the rest of us. All twelve-year-old dragons participate in the Skylight Dance. I have faith in you. You're going to succeed in time. Is there anything we can do to help?"

Davarius's ears perked up a little. "Well, maybe it would help if you two would do the exercises with me before and after school every day. I know you don't need to do them, but maybe it would be more fun to do them with someone else."

Sukkey looked at Elianora and smiled. "Of course, we can do that. No problem!" she said to him.

Elianora laughed at Sukkey's eagerness and added, "It would be our honor to help a friend."

Davarius smiled and replied, "Great! That would be fantastic. At least it wouldn't be so boring every time. Well, I'll see you both before school tomorrow then."

Elianora and Sukkey replied in unison, "See you tomorrow!" They waved goodbye and flew off toward their own homes.

Davarius started walking toward his home again with a renewed sense of hope. It was nice to have friends who were willing to help him. He'd had friends before, but they were never there after he had his accident. As he arrived at home, he greeted his mom saying,

"Guess what? Elianora and Sukkey agreed to do the exercises with me every day before and after school. Isn't that nice of them? It's great to have friends who are willing to help me."

Athien replied, "I'm so glad. You're actually smiling. I haven't seen you do that all week. And I agree. It is nice to have friends who are there for you when you need them and trust you to be there for them when they need you. That's a true friend."

As the stars came out that night, Davarius felt tired but not as discouraged as he had before.

I hope I get stronger soon, he thought as he headed to his room to sleep. Tomorrow was going to be a good day; he could just feel it.

*****

The next morning, Sukkey and Elianora arrived at school before Davarius. Even Mr. Ferrix hadn't arrived yet. Elianora turned to Sukkey and said, "Well, I guess we're a little too early."

Sukkey shrugged her shoulders and replied, "I guess so. Someone should be here any minute. Maybe we should sit over there in the shade and wait."

Elianora agreed, saying, "I bet I can beat you there without flying."

They both started running to the tree. She was right; Elianora got there first. As they sat down in the shade, they both giggled. It wasn't even five minutes until Mr. Ferrix and then Davarius showed up.

Mr. Ferrix greeted the three dragons, saying, "Good morning. Everyone is early this morning."

Davarius explained, "They agreed to do my exercises with me before and after school every day. I thought maybe it would be less boring if I had company."

Mr. Ferrix replied, "Sounds like a good idea. I want to see how strong you're getting, so I'm going to watch you this morning and see if we can make some small changes to move this along."

Elianora and Sukkey joined Davarius in the field, making sure they were far enough apart to stretch out their wings without bumping into one another. First, they started with the warm-up exercises for five minutes. Elianora noticed Davarius was able to do them easily. She and Sukkey followed his lead.

After five minutes, Mr. Ferrix called out, "Next, let's see you do the stretches. Be sure to extend your wing as far as you can and then tuck it against your side as tightly as possible."

Davarius complied. Elianora was standing on the side with his injured wing. She watched as he was able to extend his wing almost fully. She followed his movements with her own wing. Then they both tucked their wings against their sides.

Sukkey watched Elianora and Davarius as she did the stretches with them. It was easy for her and Elianora to do these stretches, but she could tell it was still slightly difficult for Davarius. He was scrunching his face slightly as he concentrated on the stretches.

Mr. Ferrix timed the three dragons, and when ten minutes went by, he said, "Okay, that's enough for now." He walked over to Davarius and had him stretch out his wing again and hold it in position for one minute. Davarius's wing trembled slightly, but he was able to keep his wing extended for the entire minute. Then Mr. Ferrix instructed, "That was amazing. Now tuck the wing and hold it for another minute."

Davarius followed his instructions and tucked his wing tightly against his side.

Elianora thought, *He's doing it! Amazing! Those two minutes seemed to creep by slowly.*

Mr. Ferrix finally said, "Okay. Time's up. Do you mind if I examine your wing for just a minute?"

Davarius replied, "Sure, I don't mind if you touch my wing."

Mr. Ferrix gently felt the bones in his wing and then examined the patches in the membrane of his wing. "It looks great. The leather patches on your membranes are healed, and the bones are strong. I think it's time to add some additional sessions and one more exercise for this week."

Davarius answered, "That's awesome. I'm ready."

Elianora and Sukkey stepped back and watched as Mr. Ferrix stood in front of Davarius and showed him the new exercise. As he showed him, Mr. Ferrix explained, "Each session, I still want you to start with the warm-up exercises for five minutes. Then do the stretching exercises for ten minutes. After that, I want you to do the new exercise I just showed you for five minutes. Be sure to do it slowly and really focus on the movement of your wing. Remember, you start with the wing tucked tightly to your side and then slowly extend it fully. Move it up and then down. Lastly, pull it back to your side and tuck it as tightly as you can against your side. You should be able to do ten repetitions in five minutes. Okay, let me see you try the new exercise."

Davarius replied, "Sure." As he tucked his wing to his side, Elianora noticed a look of determination on his face. He did the exercise ten times and finished with a smile. "I think I've got it," he said.

Mr. Ferrix encouraged him, "I believe you know exactly what to do. Now I want you to do this five times a day with at least two hours between sessions. I'll let Mr. Kristone and Ms. Emelina know you need to do them during classes. I'm sure they won't mind. I'll explain why, and I'm sure they'll be happy to help. Be sure you always move away from the class so you don't interrupt."

Davarius answered, "Thank you. I'll be sure to work hard. I just hope I can get stronger soon. I get so tired after doing the exercises, but my wing does seem to be getting a little stronger."

Mr. Ferrix replied, "I agree. Your wing is stronger. Getting tired is normal. It will get less tiring as you get used to using your wing again. You're doing a great job." He turned to Elianora and Sukkey and said, "Thank you both for being such good friends. It always helps when you have someone to support you and work out with you."

Elianora and Sukkey both smiled. Elianora said, "We're happy to help."

For the next week, the three friends worked together as Davarius faithfully completed his exercise routine five times a day. At the end of the week, Davarius seemed frustrated.

Elianora asked him, "Are you okay? You seem kind of down or frustrated."

Davarius responded, "I'm really frustrated. My wing just doesn't seem any stronger. I've done what I was supposed to do, and it doesn't feel like it's working. I need some time alone. I'm going for a walk. I'll see you guys tomorrow. Thanks for helping me." He walked away with his head down and disappeared into the nearby trees.

Elianora turned to Sukkey and said, "I hope he's okay. I don't know what to say to help him."

Sukkey replied, "Me either. I guess he just has to work it out in his head for himself. I don't think we can do that for him." The two dragons said their goodbyes and flew away.

Davarius walked through the trees listening to the sounds of the animals moving and the birds chirping. He watched two birds fly up into a tree. "You make it look so easy," he said to the birds. "I don't think I'm going to be able to fly. When I think about flying, all I see is my crash in my head. I just don't think I can overcome that. I get a knot in my stomach, and then I start shaking and I just can't bring myself to even consider that I'll ever be able to fly again. I don't know how I'm going to explain how I'm feeling to Sukkey and Elianora. Or even Mr. Ferrix, for that matter. They've all worked so hard to help me, but I just don't think I can do it."

Chapter 10

Elianora and Sukkey landed in the school yard in unison. As usual it was a bright, sunny day with fluffy clouds overhead. They both walked toward Mr. Ferrix and Davarius who were talking together. Mr. Ferrix looked up as they came near. "Good morning, Elianora and Sukkey," he said cheerfully.

Elianora smiled and said, "Good morning."

Sukkey chimed in, "Good morning."

Davarius turned toward them and said, "It's a beautiful day, isn't it?"

Elianora responded, "Yes, it is a gorgeous day. We get to enjoy beautiful days most of the time. This time of year, it doesn't rain too often. Two months from now, it will be raining almost every day. That's why we enjoy so many luscious fruits and vegetables. So how is your wing doing today?"

Davarius thought for a moment. Finally, he answered, "It's getting stronger, but I don't think it's strong enough to even glide yet."

Mr. Ferrix interrupted, "Not yet. By the end of this week, we'll try out a few hop flights to test the strength of the muscles and the membrane of your wing. That gives you this week to get as strong as you can."

Davarius shook his head and said, "I'm ready. My wing is so much stronger now than it was two weeks ago. By the end of the week, I'll be ready to try to get myself off the ground."

Mr. Ferrix instructed, "Okay, this week, I want you to add another exercise to your existing routine. First, you do the warm-up for five minutes. Next, you do the stretching for ten minutes. Then you do the strengthening moves, opening and tucking your wing for ten minutes. After that, you're going to open your wing completely and then move it forward, then down, then back, and finally back to the starting position. Do this move for ten repetitions to start. When that becomes easy, add five more repetitions. When that becomes easy, add another five. Keep adding five repetitions until you get to thirty repetitions. I know that sounds like a lot by the end of the week, but I think you're strong enough to get it done. You've done a great job strengthening your wing, and hopefully, this will also go well. Continue to do these exercises five times per day with at least two hours in between each session. Let me know if you have any difficulties. Now let me see you do the entire routine. When you get to the new exercise, I'll watch to make sure you're moving your wing correctly."

Davarius stepped back, and Elianora and Sukkey stepped to the side so they were not in his way. First, he did the warm-up, then the stretching and then the open-and-tuck exercise. When it came time to do the last exercise, he hesitated.

Mr. Ferrix was watching closely and asked, "Is there something wrong?"

Davarius quickly answered, "No, no problem." He opened his wing and began the movements. As he moved through them, he seemed to be having fun. He moved his wing effortlessly for ten repetitions. "That was easy," he said to Mr. Ferrix.

"I see that. Try doing five more," Mr. Ferrix encouraged.

Davarius did five more repetitions and then asked, "Can I try five more?"

Mr. Ferrix answered, "Okay, but no more than five more."

Davarius completed the five additional repetitions. "Now my wing is getting a little tired. I guess twenty repetitions will work."

Mr. Ferrix thought for a moment and finally replied, "Twenty repetitions to start is okay. But if you get sore or tired, then back down to fifteen for a few days. You don't want to overwork your wing too soon. By the end of the week, you should easily be up to thirty repetitions five times a day."

Elianora spoke up. "Sukkey and I can do the exercises with you after school. I'd offer to do them during school, but I'm pretty sure our teachers wouldn't want three of us to be doing exercises during classes for over thirty minutes."

Sukkey gave Elianora a look of surprise and added, "Sure, I'd love to help. Thanks for volunteering me." She and Elianora giggled together.

Davarius smiled at his two friends giggling. "That would be wonderful," he said. As the three dragons headed to class, Davarius tried to focus on what was going on around him. He was really struggling inside. He thought, *This is it. One more week, and I'm going to have to face my fears. I must try to fly. I don't want to spend the rest of my life walking everywhere. But when I think about flying, my heart starts beating fast, and I start to panic. I just have to stay calm and take that first flight carefully. I guess it's kinda like when I was first learning to fly. Just hop up and flap those wings. Sounds easy. Why is it so hard for me to do?*

Ms. Emelina and Mr. Kristone did their best to keep the young dragons' attention. With only four weeks to go until the end of school and the performance of the Skylight Dance, the dragons were all having trouble focusing on anything else. It happens like this every year. After all, the Skylight Dance is one of the biggest events in a dragon's youth. Mr. Ferrix kept them all busy with practicing the dance. They were all eager to practice again and again so they could perform the dance for their families perfectly.

After school, Elianora and Sukkey walked with Davarius away from the dragons who were still talking before leaving school. Elianora noticed Dranex watching her while he was talking with Theadosia and Anthony. When he saw her paying attention, he quickly looked back to his sister, who was talking loudly and waving her arms around. Elianora shook her head. They were definitely up to something, but she didn't know what. She tried not to think about it. Right now, she needed to help Davarius. Once he started practice flights, she would have time to talk to them and find out what was going on in their heads.

Davarius, Elianora, and Sukkey lined up far enough apart to keep from bumping each other and started the exercise routine. When they got to the new movements, it took Elianora and Sukkey a few repetitions to get the movements correct. The movements were a little different from the wing movements when they were flying. They seemed easier to Elianora. When they finished the twenty repetitions, the three of them huddled together.

Elianora asked, "So how does your wing feel now? You've done three sessions today. Is it getting tired yet?"

Davarius answered, "A little bit, but not as much as when I started the other exercises."

Sukkey interrupted, "I've got to get going. I'll talk to you guys tomorrow. Good luck with the rest of your sessions tonight." She hugged Elianora and flew off.

Davarius watched Sukkey effortlessly fly high into the sky. He sighed and turned to Elianora and asked, "Can I share something with you?"

Elianora shrugged her shoulders and answered, "Sure, is everything okay?"

Davarius could feel his heartbeat speeding up. He took a deep breath and said, "First, thank you again for helping me. It really means a lot to me to have you and Sukkey as friends. I want you to understand I'm doing my best, but I'm not sure if I'll be able to fly."

Elianora replied, "Of course, you will. Your wing is getting so much stronger. You're going to make it in time for the Skylight Dance."

Davarius took another deep breath and started to explain. "My wing is stronger, but I'm really struggling with the memory of crashing. I can remember every detail of waking up in the healer's den and feeling the pain. I was glad to be alive, but I was sure I would never be able to fly again. Now that I think I might be able to fly, it terrifies me. I start sweating, and my heart starts racing. It's like all I want to do is run away. Just the thought of flying and crashing again takes over my excitement. I feel like I'm going to disappoint everyone, especially you."

Elianora looked into Davarius's eyes and softly said, "No, you're not going to disappoint me. I'm sure it's scary to think about flying again. I'm so sorry you're struggling. Remember, just flying doesn't mean you'll crash again. You told me yourself you crashed because you took a crazy risk. Now you're more mature, and you learned from your mistake. Have you talked to your mom or maybe Mr. Ferrix about how you're feeling?"

Davarius looked down at the ground and replied, "No. My mom would just worry. I guess maybe Mr. Ferrix might know what to do to help me. I am kind of embarrassed to tell him."

Mr. Ferrix walked up to them and asked, "Tell me what?"

Davarius jerked his head up. He hadn't noticed Mr. Ferrix walking toward them. He answered, "Well, it's difficult to explain. I'm having flashbacks of my crash, and I don't know what to do about them."

Mr. Ferrix spoke quietly, saying, "Davarius, it's not unusual for someone who's been through such a severe crash like yours to have flashbacks. Do you start sweating, or does your heart start beating faster?"

Davarius responded, "Yes, both. I just want to run away. I don't think I can do this. I'm sorry I've wasted everyone's time. I just can't do this." He started walking away quickly, heading into the forest.

Elianora started to go after him, but Mr. Ferrix stopped her.

He said, "No, Elianora. Let him have some time alone. You can check on him in ten or fifteen minutes. Right now, he needs time to calm down and sort this out for himself. That may take much longer than getting his wing ready to fly."

Elianora sighed and said, "Okay. I'm going to go home and let my mom know what's going on, and then I'm going to follow him and see if there's any way I can help."

Mr. Ferrix nodded and said, "Sure. Sometimes just talking about how you're feeling can really help. He may need to talk to someone who's had a similar experience and been able to recover. I'll work on finding a dragon to help while you work on listening to Davarius. I'll let you know tomorrow what I've found after I discuss it with Davarius. See you tomorrow."

Elianora replied, "Okay, see you tomorrow." She flew away toward home. When she arrived at home, her mom and dad weren't around. Kizzie and Nonie weren't home either. She looked around and finally found Stepharus.

Stepharus greeted her with a hug. "What's the matter?" he asked. "You seem upset. Can I help?"

Elianora sat down by the firepit. Stepharus joined her and waited quietly for her to explain. Elianora began. "You remember the dragon I told you about that you rescued after he crashed on Pyreton Island?"

Stepharus answered, "Sure. Davarius is his name, right?"

Elianora continued, "Right. Well, he's been working hard to strengthen his wing so he can fly or at least glide in the Skylight Dance. His wing is getting much stronger, but now he's getting scared. He told me he has flashbacks. His heartbeat gets faster, and he starts to sweat. Then after he told Mr. Ferrix what was going on, he ran off into the forest. I want to go find him and talk to him, but I don't know what to say."

Stepharus thought quietly for a minute and then replied, "Elianora, you don't need to say anything. You're his friend, so you just need to listen. Try to get him to talk about how he feels. Don't try to fix what he's feeling or tell him how to feel. He may need to talk to a dragon that has been through something similar."

Elianora interrupted. "That's what Mr. Ferrix said. He's working on finding a dragon to help."

Stepharus continued, "I think I know just the right dragon. You go find Davarius and listen to him. I'll go talk to this dragon and ask if he'll help. Then I'll go talk to Mr. Ferrix. It's going to be okay, Elianora. You just be a good friend and let the adults help."

Elianora wiped away some tears and said, "Okay, I'm going to find Davarius. Can you tell Mom and Dad where I am and let them know I'll be home as soon as I can, but it might be later than usual?"

Stepharus responded, "Absolutely, I'll let you know what I find out when you get back tonight."

Elianora said over her shoulder as she prepared to fly away, "Okay. Thanks, Stepharus. You're the best brother ever!" She flew away heading for the forest. As she found the forest where Davarius had disappeared, she flew closer to the tops of the trees. She listened intently to see if she could hear any twigs snapping or leaves crunching. Finally, she could see a lake, and she noticed Davarius walking around the lake. She landed close to the trees and started walking toward him. As she got closer, she called out, "Davarius, can I talk to you?"

Davarius turned and looked at Elianora. "Yeah, sure. I don't know what more I can say, but I'll gladly listen."

Elianora caught up to him, and they both sat down on the shore of the lake. She said quietly, "I really don't know exactly what to say. I'd rather be the one that listens. I want to help, but I don't know exactly how. I'm a good listener though."

Davarius chuckled and responded, "Okay. I'm sorry I just ran away, but I needed to get away by myself for a while. I found this lake when we first moved to Loopdy Island, and ever since, it's the place I go when I need to think. Like I told you, I'm scared to fly ever again. I don't know if I can trust myself not to make another stupid decision. I know my body is healed, and it may be physically possible to fly, but I get scared just thinking about it. How am I going to actually do it?"

Elianora thought for a moment and then replied, "Well, I guess you talk to yourself and remember that you've worked hard to get strong and healthy. You know that you made a bad decision. But you've learned from that. We all make mistakes, but we do our best to figure out what went wrong and why we made that choice. Then we forgive ourselves and do what we need to do even if we are scared."

Davarius looked into Elianora's eyes. "You know something? You're the first person that I told how scared I was. I figured you would be mad after all the trouble you've gone to. But instead, you're here sitting in my quiet place with me understanding. If you can do that, then I can find a way to conquer my fears, I think. But I know it's going to be easy to say and hard to do. Every time I think about jumping off the ground, my thoughts go to my crash and my pain. Then I start thinking about how I'm letting everyone around me down."

Elianora waited quietly for a few minutes without saying anything.

Davarius broke the silence by saying, "I guess I'll remind myself that part of my journey is over, and I survived. I've come so far with my recovery. I don't want to stop now. But when you see me shaking before I take that first hop, just remember you're the one who listened and got me to take the next steps."

Elianora replied, "I will. I know you'll be flying soon. I talked to my brother, Stepharus, about what I should do, and he said he might know a dragon that had a similar experience to yours. He's going to talk to him and see if he can help you. Maybe hearing about his journey will give you the courage to continue your own journey."

Davarius nodded and said, "That would be nice. He might understand how I'm feeling and what I'm going through. Maybe he'll have some ideas about how to move past this."

Elianora responded, "I bet he will. You know, it occurs to me that you may always have flashbacks, but when you fly again, you'll be able to put them in a safe place where they won't be so scary. I don't think you'll ever forget your crash or the surgeries and the recovery. But once you make it, you can look back and realize how strong you are and how far you've come from the crazy young dragon who took that crazy risk. Can I make a suggestion?"

Davarius nodded. "Of course, what is it?"

Elianora smiled and said, "Maybe you should start this process by talking to your mom and letting her know how you're feeling. I'm sure she would want to help in any way she can. Of all the dragons on this planet, I would guess she loves you the most."

Davarius chuckled and replied, "Yes, she does. She's been so great through all this. You're right. I'll tell her tonight. Well, it's getting late. I guess we should both get home."

Elianora laughed with him and said, "You're right. But I'm walking with you instead of flying. I want you to realize you're not alone anymore. And when you start thinking that you are alone, I want you to look back on today and realize that's just not true."

As they walked toward Davarius's home and talked, they watched the sun go down, and the stars start to fill the night sky. The moon was bright and full. When they arrived at his home, Elianora turned and said to him, "Thank you for trusting me with your secret. I know that had to be hard to admit to anyone. I'll see you tomorrow at school."

Davarius waved goodbye as he watched Elianora fly toward her home. His mom rushed out to greet him. She was so happy to see him safe.

Chapter 11

Elianora was anxious to speak with Stepharus to see if he had spoken to the dragon he mentioned.

"Good morning," she greeted Stepharus.

"Good morning," Stepharus answered with a smile. "I tried to speak to the dragon I was thinking could help Davarius and found out he is off on business. He's not going to be back for a few months. Is there another dragon you know of that has had an accident and would be willing to talk with Davarius?"

Elianora thought for a moment. "The only dragon I can think of is Dranex. When he was six years old, he fell and broke his back leg. Sukkey, Theadosia, and I flew him to safety. I hadn't thought of that in a long time. I guess it wouldn't hurt to ask him."

Stepharus put his paw on Elianora's shoulder. "I remember that now. He wasn't as badly hurt as Davarius, but I'd bet he can relate to the way Davarius is feeling."

Elianora nodded. "I'll ask him and see what he says. I better get going to school. Hopefully, Dranex will be there a little early today so I can talk to him. See you later," she called over her shoulder as she leapt into the air, "and thank you for your help."

*****

Elianora landed in the clearing close to school looking for Davarius or Dranex, but neither dragon was there yet. She walked toward the class area and looked around to find Dranex as soon as he arrived. After just a few minutes, she saw Theadosia, Anthony, and Dranex flying toward her.

Dranex landed close by and greeted her cheerfully. "Good morning, Elianora. How are you today?"

Elianora walked closer to Dranex and answered, "Good morning. I'm fine. Can I ask you something in private, please?"

Dranex was quiet for a moment. Finally, he responded, "Sure, what's up?"

As the two of them walked a short distance away from the other dragons, Elianora began. "Do you remember when you broke your leg?"

Dranex carefully replied, "Yes, I remember. Why?"

Elianora continued. "I was wondering if you would be willing to talk with Davarius about how you felt when that happened and afterward how you found the courage to fly again."

Dranex smiled and said, "That was a long time ago, but I guess I could talk to him. I don't know if that would be very helpful. I wasn't hurt nearly as bad as he was, and it didn't take me long to heal and get back up into the sky."

Elianora smiled back and replied, "Thank you. I'll talk to Davarius and see if he'd be willing to talk with you about your injury and recovery. I think it might help him right now to know he's not alone. Don't sugarcoat how you felt please. He needs to hear how difficult it was at first and how you found the courage and strength to take off on those first few flights."

Dranex nodded and said, "I get it. I'll be honest about how scary it was to fly and then land those first few times."

Elianora clapped her paws together and looked around for Davarius. "There he is," she said, mostly to herself, "I'll tell him and see if he can talk to you right now." She walked quickly away toward Davarius.

Davarius smiled as she approached him. "Well, you look like a dragon on a mission. What are you up to this morning?"

Elianora tried to control her excitement. She took a deep breath and asked Davarius, "Would you be willing to talk to Dranex?"

Davarius looked puzzled. "Uh, sure, what would I be talking to Dranex about?"

Elianora realized she wasn't explaining herself clearly. "Oh, sorry. So I remembered that when we were six years old, Dranex broke his back leg, and we had to fly him out to safety. I was thinking that maybe he would understand how you're feeling about starting to fly again. I asked him if he'd be willing to tell you about it, and he said yes. Don't worry, I didn't say anything about what you told me. He just thinks you're a little anxious about flying again."

Davarius nodded and noticed Dranex walking toward him. "Here he comes. No time like the present, I guess."

Dranex walked up and shook Davarius's paw. "So I guess Elianora told you about my accident years ago. She thought maybe I could tell you how I was feeling and how I got the courage to get back into the air. Is now a good time?"

Davarius said, "Sure. How about we talk over here?" He pointed a short distance away. "I'd love to hear about your experience."

Elianora noticed Sukkey heading toward her and walked quickly to meet her as Davarius and Dranex walked away together.

Sukkey stopped and asked Elianora, "Why are the two of them talking? They never talk together without other dragons around. What's going on?"

Elianora hushed her and then whispered, "Dranex agreed to talk to Davarius about his accident when we were young. I thought it might help to hear how another dragon got hurt and then found the courage to fly again. Come on, let's go sit down over there and let them talk. But not too far away. I want to see what happens."

Sukkey joined Elianora as she walked a short distance away and sat down. "I feel like I missed something. You'll have to fill me in later." The two friends sat quietly, watching Dranex and Davarius talking together. They seemed to be deep in conversation.

Dranex explained the details of how he broke his leg and how the three dragons flew him to safety. "That was scary, but not the scariest part. Once my leg healed, which really didn't take long, I had to get back to flying. At first, I was being pompous, walking around telling any dragon that would listen that it was no big deal. Then came the day I had to take off into the air. I was shaking, and I was sweating and breathing hard. It was crazy, like my body just wouldn't cooperate with my brain. I wanted to take off and glide around, but when I tried, I just couldn't make myself do it."

Davarius nodded and interjected, "I know how you feel. Logically, I want to just fly. But when I think about doing it, I start shaking and sweating too."

Dranex continued, "Right. It doesn't seem like it should be so hard, but it really is hard. I kept thinking about how I crashed and how my leg hurt so much. If those three dragons hadn't been there, who knows how long I would have laid on the ground hurt and unable to get help. But I have to tell you, I finally decided that there was no magic to get me back to flying. I had to take small hops and glide even if I was shaking and scared. I took a deep breath and did it. At first, I didn't fly, mostly just hopped up and landed. But I kept trying, and after several attempts, I finally flew a short distance. When I landed, I didn't crash, and I was safe. That was a rush. I think it was the greatest flight I've ever had. I did it without any other dragon's help. After that, I felt less scared, and I just kept taking short flights. After a week or so, I got enough courage to fly high up and take flight for a longer journey. It was amazing. Since then, I don't think about being afraid. I just hop into the air and go. I'm sure you will be able to fly soon. You're strong and brave. Besides, if you need a friend to fly with you, I'm here anytime. Just let me know. Oh, and don't tell any other dragons about what I just told you. That's between us survivors."

Davarius shook Dranex's paw and said, "Thanks, fellow survivor. It's nice to know someone else who gets how I'm feeling. I'd really like us to fly together someday soon. Once I'm strong enough to get off the ground."

Dranex and Davarius walked toward the other dragons talking together. Mr. Ferrix called the class together and got them all lined up and warmed up so they could practice the dance routine. Davarius followed Mr. Ferrix over to the side so he could work on his exercise routine.

Once he was done, Davarius asked Mr. Ferrix, "Well, what now?"

Mr. Ferrix answered, "Today I'd like to see you try some hop flights. What I want to see is you hop up as if you're taking off and spread your wings, then land. Let me see you try that for the first time."

Davarius took a deep breath. He could feel himself trembling. He was determined to do this anyway, no matter how scared he really was. The first hop he didn't spread his wings.

Mr. Ferrix encouraged him, saying, "That's a start. Now this time, try opening those wings at the same time."

Davarius shook his head and backed up a short distance. He thought, *You can do this. You're strong enough. Do it even though you're terrified. You can do this.* He started a short run, then hopped, and spread his wings. As his feet landed safely back on the ground, he could hear Elianora, Dranex, Sukkey, and Anthony cheering, "Way to go, Davarius!"

He took another deep breath and turned to see Mr. Ferrix clapping and walking in his direction. "Nice, very nice for a dragon who hasn't flown for such a long time. I'm very impressed."

Davarius smiled and turned to go back to his starting place and try again. He wasn't shaking anymore, and he could feel a rush of confidence come over him. He looked at Mr. Ferrix and took a short run and hopped as he opened his wings.

Mr. Ferrix called out to Davarius, "Okay, now I want to see how many times in a row you can hop and fly."

Davarius walked back to his starting position and took several deep breaths. He ran, then hopped, and finally flew and landed. Then he did it again. On the first try, he did it three times before needing to rest. He turned toward Mr. Ferrix and said, "I can do better, just give me a minute to catch my breath."

Mr. Ferrix replied, "Sure. You're doing great. Nice job, you've got this."

Davarius took off again, and this time, he was able to do it five times in a row. He walked back to his starting place and started again. When he hopped, something went wrong, and he fell on his hurt wing. He could hear the total silence all around him. He knew all the dragons were watching him. He stood up, dusted himself off, and stretched out his wing. He was fine. He walked back to the starting point and took off again. This time, he was able to do ten flights in a row. He could hear all the dragons cheering and clapping as he landed and took off again. When he landed the tenth time, he felt like he was stronger than he had ever been before. He said, *I did it. I'm going to be able to fly again. I can't believe it. I did it.*

Mr. Ferrix ended class and sent the dragons on their way except for Davarius. Elianora, Sukkey, Dranex, and Anthony walked toward him while Theadosia stood to the side listening. They were all excited and talking all at once. Mr. Ferrix waited for them to congratulate Davarius and then interrupted, "You did wonderful today, Davarius." He turned to the group of dragons and added, "This group gives me great hope for the future of dragons. It's great to see you support one another. Great job, all of you!"

The dragons soon left, leaving Elianora and Davarius to walk alone together. Davarius turned to Mr. Ferrix and said, "I want to try flying up to the rock cliff. I believe I can do it now."

Mr. Ferrix replied, "Well, you seemed to do well, and even when you fell, you kept going. If you want to try, I'll be here to catch you if you need me to."

Davarius turned to Elianora and said, "Here I go." He took a deep breath and started to hop into the air. As his feet left the ground, he spread his wings wide open. He could feel the air current lift him up into the sky. He began to flap his wings gently at first. Then as he gained momentum, he flapped his wings even stronger. He could feel the air rush past his face. He had forgotten the thrill of flying. The adrenaline rushed through his whole body as he continued to move his wings in a strong motion. He looked toward the rock cliff and realized he was already halfway there. He made a slight dive toward the ground and flapped his wings as hard as he could as he sailed upward again. His heart was pounding, and he flashed back to his crash, just for a moment. He shook his head and focused on the air current lifting him up toward his goal. As he approached the rock cliff, he put out his feet and tilted his wings for a gentle, perfect landing. He felt a huge rush of excitement run through him. He folded his wings and turned around to look at Elianora and Mr. Ferrix, who were both standing on the ground clapping. He leapt off the cliff and spread his wings into the air current. He let it carry him as he glided down to the ground and landed carefully near Elianora.

Mr. Ferrix proudly announced, "Great job, Davarius! You had an amazing flight. I'm very proud of you."

Elianora congratulated Davarius and asked, "How did you find the courage to fly so quickly?"

Davarius smiled and answered, "I talked with my mom last night, and then I listened to Dranex explain what had happened to him. It made me realize that being afraid was no reason to stop trying. I made up my mind that I was going to keep working and moving forward until I can glide and fly for the Skylight Dance. I was really shaking and scared, but I just did what I could anyway. Once I was successful, that gave me more courage. Although when I fell on my wing, I was worried. I thought I was done for good. But once I got up and stretched out my wing, I realized I was okay. My wing is stronger than I thought. It felt so good to spread my wings and fly, even if it was for just a few seconds. It was a rush of joy and power. That's what encouraged me to try to fly up to the rock cliff."

Elianora patted Davarius on the shoulder. "You are amazing! Watching you keep trying again and again, I realized you are going to be able to be part of the Skylight Dance, just like we planned. Then I watched you fly up to the rock cliff and glide back down with ease. It was so amazing! All the dragons are so excited. This will be the best Skylight Dance ever performed on Loopdy Island."

As they walked, Davarius asked Elianora, "Hey, do you have time to go to the meadow and have a fizzy juice with me?"

Elianora laughed and said, "Of course, that sounds delicious. We haven't had fizzy juice in weeks. Let's try mango and strawberry this time. Sound good?"

They turned and walked toward the meadow. After gathering the fruit and fizzy water, they sat together on a bench and enjoyed their fizzy juice. Davarius sighed and said to Elianora, "Thank you. I don't know if I would have been able to get through this without you being my friend. I was worried when you said Dranex wanted to talk to me. I figured he was going to say something mean. But instead, he opened up to me, and what he said really helped me. I guess there's more kindness in him than I thought at first. When all the dragons started cheering and clapping, I was stunned. I didn't think they really cared if I was able to fly, but when they did that, I realized they were glad I had succeeded. Today has been a really encouraging day. And I was ready to just give up and stop trying. Your encouragement and friendship have really made a difference in my life. Thank you again."

Elianora smiled. "Well, I really wanted you to be part of the Skylight Dance. I knew you had it in you to be able to fly one day. I just didn't realize it was going to be today! You're right. Dranex has a better side. He just seems to hide behind the tough dragon mask. But once you get to know him, he's really a great dragon. I'm glad he was able to encourage you. I can't wait to see the faces of all the adult dragons when they see you fly up to that rock cliff and then glide back down and join the rest of us at the end of the dance. It's going to be amazing."

Davarius finished his juice and stood. "Can I take your glass and put it in the tray?"

Elianora responded, "Yes, that would be nice. Thank you!"

Davarius put the dirty glasses in the tray and rejoined Elianora. "We better head home now. I need to practice five more times today. My mom will be so surprised when she sees me hop and fly."

Elianora walked next to Davarius and said, "I'm sure she will be so excited. No one knew for sure whether you would be able to fly again. Now you know for sure, and I got to witness your very first flight."

They said their goodbyes as Elianora left Davarius at his home and flew away. She headed home, and as she was flying, she noticed Dranex flying alone not far away. She flew over to him and shouted, "Hey! I wanted to thank you for sharing your story with Davarius. I think you really helped him."

Dranex shouted back, "You're welcome. Glad I could help. It felt great to help another dragon."

Elianora responded, "I'll see you tomorrow. Thanks again." She headed home, and when she landed, she could see Stepharus and Nonie sitting around the firepit. "Hi! Guess what happened today?"

Stepharus responded, "What happened today?"

Elianora rushed to explain. "Davarius was able to hop and fly. It was amazing. Dranex spoke with him, and I don't know exactly what he said, but then Davarius just started trying, and before long, he was hopping and flying. He fell on his wing once, but he just got up and tried again. The whole class cheered and clapped."

Nonie replied, "That's wonderful. I can't believe he was able to fly, even a little bit. His injury was severe, wasn't it?"

Elianora realized it was supposed to be a surprise. She whispered to her siblings, "It's amazing, but it's a secret. Don't tell anyone."

Stepharus and Nonie both laughed with Elianora.

Finally, Nonie replied, "Your secret is safe with me!"

Stepharus chimed in, "And me too. I won't tell another dragon. It should be a big surprise when he is able to fly for the Skylight Dance."

Elianora sat down and said, "It will be amazing. I can't wait until the Skylight Dance is here. It's only a few more weeks. This will be the best Skylight Dance any dragon has ever seen."

*****

Meanwhile, Davarius sat at home with his mom. He explained, "I was able to hop and fly today. I did it ten times in a row. I need to practice five more series of ten times. Yesterday I was ready to give up. I didn't think I would be able to ever fly again. Then Dranex, of all dragons, told me about how he was hurt when he was young and how he was able to fly again even though he was really scared. I realized it was okay to be scared. I just couldn't let that stop me from trying until I was able to fly. It was an amazing day!"

Athien hugged him and said, "I knew you could do it. You have gotten so much stronger lately. Before you had your accident, you didn't listen very well. Now you listen and think about other dragons. You've grown into a better dragon since then. I'm so proud of you, Davarius. You've learned some very important lessons since your accident. You're going to grow up and be an amazing dragon someday."

Chapter 12

Elianora and Sukkey got up early on the day of the Skylight Dance. They worked most of the day to make sure they looked especially beautiful for their big event. They helped each other make sure each scale was polished and shiny. As the sun began to fade and the stars began to shine brightly in the sky, they flew together to meet at the meadow where they would perform in just a few hours. Mr. Ferrix quietly watched as the young dragons laughed and chatted excitedly. All the preparations had been made for the Skylight Dance. He counted the young dragons to be sure all twenty-one of them were here and ready to go.

Mr. Ferrix cleared his throat and announced, "Each of you needs to spread out and stretch so you're warmed up and ready to perform. Your families will start arriving any time now along with the rest of the dragons on the island."

Each of the dragons moved a slight distance from the dragons around them and stretched. Dranex finished stretching and pranced over to Anthony and Theadosia. "This is going to be wonderful!" he declared.

Anthony replied, "We are young. She may say no."

Dranex looked at Anthony and assured him, "She will say yes. I just know it. Besides, you and Theadosia are together, and you're the same age as I am."

Theadosia interjected, "I'm sure she'll say yes. I wish you luck, brother."

Across the meadow, Elianora stood next to Davarius and Sukkey. She asked Davarius, "How are you feeling today?"

Davarius answered, "I feel great. I'm a little nervous because I don't want to let everyone down. But I know I'll be able to fly up to the rock cliff with no problem."

Sukkey replied, "You'll do great. This is going to be the most spectacular Skylight Dance that has ever been performed on Loopdy Island."

Mr. Ferrix clapped his paws to get the young dragons' attention. They quieted down to hear what he had to say to them. He began. "Okay, every dragon in their assigned place. Be sure to keep walking around in your place to keep your muscles ready to fly. The families are now arriving, and we will begin in just a few minutes when the crowd gets settled."

Each of the young dragons took their place in the meadow. The sound of excitement filled the air. They could hear their family members laughing and talking with all the other dragons. Elianora's heart was beating so fast she could feel it in her throat. Dranex stood on the other side of the meadow watching Elianora as she paced quietly back and forth.

Mr. Ferrix took his place in front of the row of young dragons. He announced to the crowd, "Welcome everyone to this year's Skylight Dance. We have an amazing performance ready to delight you." The crowd clapped in unison. Mr. Ferrix turned to face the young dragons and signaled for the music to begin.

As the music started playing a solemn drumbeat with a chorus humming in the background, the dragons took their places and faced the audience. Davarius stood in the center of the young dragons. The dragons on each side of him stepped forward and turned before taking off into the air. Then the next pair of dragons followed by stepping forward and taking flight. Each pair of dragons did the same movement as they began to weave into the pattern they practiced. Finally, Dranex and Elianora, who were at the end of the lines, took flight. Dranex and Elianora flew toward each other and joined the group of dragons as they all began to weave back and forth while the starlight glinted off their scales. They looked like a giant dragon's tail flipping back and forth in the sky. As the first dragons reached the loopdy loops, they began, one by one, weaving their way through the loopdy loops and then flying downward to land in their original places. The music continued to play as each dragon took their turn flying through the loopdy loops and landing. Finally, Dranex and Elianora reached their turn, and Elianora flew into the loopdy loops first. As she emerged, she saw Dranex enter the loopdy loops and emerge to join her in the sky before they landed at the same time in their places.

The music changed to a waltz; the dragons began flying back into the sky in pairs. Each pair of dragons took flight and then flew up to their position in the sky and began to dance with each other. Finally, Dranex and Elianora took flight. As they took flight, Davarius also took flight between them. The three of them flew into the air, and then Davarius broke off and flew over to the rock cliff and landed gracefully. Dranex and Elianora flew to their places. Davarius began to dance to the music on the rock cliff. Fireworks began to explode all around the dragons as the music turned to an upbeat, triumphant rhythm. The pairs of young dragons danced circling each other in the sky as the music played a hopeful melody. The fireworks were in green, blue, red, and yellow and the rainbow of colors glistened across the scales of the young dragons with every flash. The audience watched as the symphony of lights created by the fireworks glistening off their scales seemed to weave around them.

Dranex took a deep breath and turned to Elianora as they were dancing, holding her claws and asked, "Elianora, will you be my girlfriend?"

Elianora kept swaying to the music, but her ears couldn't comprehend the sound of the music or the fireworks going off around her. The world seemed at a standstill. She blinked her eyes and looked into Dranex's eyes. He smiled at her, and she pulled her claws out of his and immediately shouted, "What? I'm only…we're only twelve years old. That is way too young to have a boyfriend. I don't even think of you that way. I don't think of any dragon that way. You are such a self-centered, red reptile. Wow."

Dranex tried to keep dancing, stunned by Elianora's reaction. He burst out, "We're not too young. Theadosia and Anthony are boyfriend and girlfriend, are they not?"

Elianora tried to keep dancing even though she just wanted to fly away. Finally, she replied, "I'm not like them. I don't want a boyfriend. Certainly not you." She stopped talking as she saw Dranex's face turn to hurt. She realized she had been very mean. Just then the music began to build as the dragons flew toward their places and landed in pairs. Dranex flew downward without Elianora. She caught up with him and saw Davarius glide from the cliff to fly in between them, and the three of them landed together in their places.

The music finished, and Mr. Ferrix stood in front of the young dragons. He announced to the cheering crowd, "Thank you all for coming!" He turned around to the young dragons and said, "Great job! You're all free to go join your families."

Elianora tried to see Dranex through the crowd of dragons as the young dragons fed into the crowd. She finally caught a glimpse of him standing apart from the other dragons, with his head looking down at the ground and a few tears dropping. He took flight and flew away before she could talk to him. She noticed Theadosia giving her a death glare as she also flew away following Dranex.

Davarius walked over to Elianora and noticed she seemed upset. He asked, "Are you okay? Is there something wrong?"

Elianora shook her head and answered, "I'm okay. You did a great job. Everything was so beautiful—the fireworks, the stars, the music, and the sight of you flying. What a wonderful night."

Davarius smiled at her as Sukkey joined them. Sukkey looked at Elianora and smiled with a knowing look. She said, "It was beautiful. That was the most spectacular Skylight Dance ever performed on Loopdy Island."

The three friends walked through the crowd to find their families. Davarius found his mom first. They hugged each other, and Athien said, "You were spectacular. I can't believe you finally flew again. I am so proud of you. Elianora, thank you for helping my son."

They walked away toward home. Davarius turned and waved goodbye to Elianora and Sukkey.

Sukkey saw her family in the distance and turned to Elianora and said, "We'll talk tomorrow. I hope you have a great evening with your family. See you then."

Elianora watched Sukkey walk away with her family and finally saw her own family. She joined them and hugged each one before they headed home. Once they arrived home, they sat around the firepit and enjoyed a wonderful dinner of roasted scallops, amaranth and cucumber salad, and roasted sweet potatoes. They laughed and talked for hours. As they all headed off to sleep, Elianora asked her mom, "Can I talk to you for a few minutes?"

Verity replied, "Of course." She turned to her husband and said, "I'll be there in a few minutes." She and Elianora moved to the firepit and she asked, "What's wrong?"

Elianora sighed and explained, "While we were up in the sky dancing, Dranex asked me to be his girlfriend. I freaked out and said no, but then I said some mean things. I called him a red reptile. I tried to explain that I was too young, but I was so flustered I just kept talking, and I know I hurt his feelings. I'm pretty sure all the other dragons heard the entire conversation. I don't know what to do." She held her head in her claws and stared at the firepit.

Verity sat quietly for a moment and then put her paw on Elianora's shoulder and said, "You're right about being too young to have a boyfriend. However, you were wrong to call Dranex names and to shout at him. I'm sure he is very hurt and disappointed. You need to apologize to him, in private, about the insults and your anger, but be sure he understands you only want to be friends. Tomorrow morning, before the graduation ceremony, you need to talk to Dranex and resolve this so you can relax and enjoy your graduation."

Elianora smiled at her mom and replied, "You're right. I shouldn't have called Dranex names, and I'm not sure why it made me angry. I guess I was just so shocked by the question. I'll find him tomorrow morning and apologize so we can both enjoy our graduation."

After a difficult night's sleep, Elianora woke early the next morning. She spoke with her mom saying, "I'm going to take care of that situation. I'll be back soon."

Verity responded, "Good. See you in a while."

Kizzie asked Verity, "What's going on with Elianora?"

Verity replied, "It's a mother's secret." She held one claw to her snout with a twinkle in her eye.

Kizzie laughed and said, "Okay, Mom."

*****

Elianora flew toward the school searching for Dranex along the way. She finally saw him sitting alone near the meadow where they had performed the Skylight Dance. As she landed, he looked up and said nothing. She walked over to him and asked, "Can I talk to you?"

Dranex looked down at the ground and responded quietly, "Sure."

Elianora began to explain, saying, "First, I'm really sorry about how I responded to your question last night. I meant what I said about being too young, but I was very wrong to call you a red reptile and to get so angry. I was just so surprised at the question. I don't think of any dragon as a boyfriend, even you. We've been friends for such a long time, I just think of you as one of my best friends."

Dranex looked up at her and said, "It's my fault anyway. I shouldn't have asked you with all the other dragons around. It was just so hurtful for you to yell at me in front of all the other dragons. I forgive you for reacting so badly."

Elianora sat down next to Dranex and asked, "Are we still friends?"

Dranex looked at her and hesitantly replied, "I'm not sure. I need time to figure that out."

Elianora nodded and said, "No problem. I'll leave you alone then. See you later at the graduation ceremony."

Dranex nodded and shrugged his shoulders. "See you then."

Elianora stood and took flight. As she headed toward Sukkey's home, she hoped that Dranex could forgive her, and they could still be friends. She thought, *It wouldn't have gone so badly if I hadn't shouted so all the other dragons could hear.*

Sukkey greeted Elianora as she landed by her home. "Good morning. How are you doing this morning?"

Elianora sighed and said, "I'm okay."

Sukkey replied, "That bad, huh?"

Elianora and Sukkey sat together under some trees. Elianora explained, "I talked to Dranex this morning and apologized to him for calling him names and shouting. But I still made sure he understood I don't want to have a boyfriend. I told him I think of him as one of my best friends. He said he needs time to think about that. It makes me sad."

Sukkey replied, "I'm sure it will be okay with time. He thought you would be as excited about being his girlfriend as he felt about being your boyfriend. It was awkward to hear the two of you as we were dancing. All the dragons were surprised he asked you, except of course, Theadosia and Anthony. I think their family just doesn't think it's a big deal. I agree with you that we are way too young to have a boyfriend."

Elianora listened quietly and finally said, "I guess you're right. His family just thinks about it differently. Hopefully he can forgive me, and we can continue to be good friends. Enough about that, are you ready for the graduation ceremony?"

Sukkey jumped up and said, "I can't wait. We get our amulets today. We are no longer dragonlings. We are now dragons."

Elianora stood up and replied, "Yes, we are. I can't wait to see my amulet. My parents have been very careful to keep it a secret. I guess we better get ready for our graduation ceremony. I'll see you there."

Sukkey waved at Elianora as she flew up into the air. "See you then!" she shouted.

As Elianora arrived home, she could sense the excitement from her whole family. "It's almost time," she said to her parents. "Don't forget the most important part."

Verity laughed and answered, "I've got it all set. I think you'll love it. Now go make sure you're ready to go. We'll leave in one hour."

Elianora headed to her room to get ready. She felt tingly as she looked into the mirror. She thought, *Next time I look at myself in the mirror, I will be wearing my amulet. I'm so excited.*

Verity called up to Elianora, "Let's go. We're all ready."

Elianora headed down to join her family. They all flew together to the meadow for the graduation ceremony. "See you soon," she said as she walked toward the group of dragons.

Mr. Ferrix walked over to the class for the last time and said, "It's graduation time. Everyone, line up in a single row. When I call your name, your parents will come up and present you with your amulet. When you're done receiving your amulet, please walk behind the line and form the line across, just like you did for the Skylight Dance so everyone can admire all of you with your amulets."

Dranex and Theadosia were the first two dragons in the line. Anthony was behind Theadosia, followed by twelve of their classmates including Theadosia's posse of friends. Davarius was next, followed by three other classmates. At the end were Sukkey and finally, Elianora. The procession music began to play as the dragons marched forward. Mr. Ferrix asked Dranex's parents to come forward and stepped to the side.

As Dranex's parents came forward, Mr. Ferrix announced, "Our first student is Dranex."

Dranex stepped forward and anxiously waited for his parents to stand next to him. Callamdon started to speak. "Dranex, your mother and I are so proud of you. We present you with your special amulet. It represents your increasing courage and strength. We have watched you grow and gain courage since you were a child." Callamdon looked over to Greta who was holding the amulet and smiling. Callamdon continued, "Your amulet is a sun of silver with a brilliant orange center and flames of red and blue. Once you were a scared, shy dragonling. Now you are a courageous dragon with the strength to face the future." As Callamdon finished speaking, Greta placed the amulet on Dranex's neck. The crowd clapped, and Dranex stepped to the side and walked behind the line of dragons with his head held high and a proud smile on his face. He took his place and waited for his parents to present Theadosia with her amulet.

Mr. Ferrix waited while Dranex walked away and then announced, "Our next student is Theadosia."

Theadosia stepped up to her parents as Callamdon started to speak. "Theadosia, your mother and I are very proud of you. We present you with your special amulet. It represents your connection with many dragons. It is a full moon with a gray crystal in the center surrounded by purple, blue, green, pink, red, yellow, orange, aqua, brown, and white crystals. This represents the variety of crystals to represent the variety of dragons you care for. You've always been able to stand against wrongdoing and yet get along with all dragons. You always help your twin brother whenever he needs you." As he finished speaking, Greta placed the amulet on Theadosia's neck. She hugged her mother strongly as tears rolled down her face and onto Greta's orange scales. After a few minutes, she let go of her mother and then turned to give her father the same big hug. The crowd clapped and kept clapping until she finally let go and walked around the line of dragons to her place in line next to her brother. Her parents proudly left the front and took their place in the crowd.

Mr. Ferrix said, "Thank you. Our next student is Anthony."

Anthony stepped forward as his parents joined him. His mother, Hazelia, stood proudly with her brown scales shining and her pink highlights sparkling. She began to speak. "Anthony, we are very proud of you and the dragon you have become. I will have your father describe your amulet." She turned to her husband, Rogar, and smiled.

Rogar stood with his shoulders back and his gold scales shimmering. He smiled and said, "Your amulet is a book with two sides. The first side has a yellow eye with a green center surrounded by purple, red, and orange crystals. The second side is a brown crystal dragon's wing surrounded by blue, pink, white, and aqua crystals. They represent your pursuit of knowledge and your desire to learn about our world. We look forward to watching you discover even more as you grow." Rogar placed the amulet over Anthony's head as his red stripes glimmered. The crowd clapped as Anthony proudly walked around the dragons, and his parents took their place in the crowd.

The dragons all stood patiently as they listened to each of the next twelve sets of parents present their dragon graduate with their special amulet. Elianora looked over the crowd to find her family and noticed her parents speaking with a teal-and-purple dragon that looked like the oldest dragon she had ever seen. She wondered who the dragon was and why he was talking to her parents. Her parents nodded as if they were agreeing to something, and the teal dragon walked away slowly, not looking at anyone. He faded into the crowd.

Finally, Mr. Ferrix announced, "Our next student is Davarius."

Davarius stepped forward as his mom joined him in front. Athien was smiling. She began to speak. "Davarius, I am so very proud of you. You have come so far since you were hurt. I thought you would never fly again. Yesterday, I was pleasantly surprised to watch you take flight once again." Tears started to roll down her cheek. She brushed them aside, as she continued to speak. She said, "Davarius, you are a miracle. Words cannot express how proud I am of you. You have so much strength and courage. Your amulet represents healing. It is a gold flower with seven petals that are emerald green. The center is a blue sapphire heart. Your connection to nature has helped you overcome your difficulties so that you can fly once again. I love you, my son." Athien hugged Davarius, as tears rolled down both their faces. The crowd clapped as Davarius walked around the line of dragons, and Athien took her place in the crowd.

Mr. Ferrix announced the next three students, and their parents presented them with their amulets. Sukkey and Elianora waited patiently for their turns. As the three dragons stepped around them to get in their places, Sukkey stepped forward.

Mr. Ferrix announced, "Our next student is Sukkey."

Sukkey's parents joined her in front of the crowd. Her mother, Fatima, stood quietly next to her with her white scales outlined by the beautiful emerald-green highlights. She started to speak. "Sukkey, we are so proud of you. Your father, Sebastian, will describe your amulet." She turned to Sebastian as she held out Sukkey's amulet.

The sturdy orange dragon at Fatima's side turned to Sukkey with his blue highlights sparkling. Sebastian said, "Sukkey, you are beautiful and strong. You have taken your time to grow into the beautiful dragon you have become. Your amulet is a pearl, which also takes time to grow into something beautiful. On the left side of the pearl are orange and purple crystals that glisten. We love you."

Fatima placed Sukkey's amulet around her neck as the crowd clapped. Sukkey hugged her parents and then walked around Elianora to take her place in line as her parents returned to the crowd.

Mr. Ferrix announced, "Finally, our last student this year is Elianora."

Elianora stepped forward, as her parents joined her in the front. Her father, Cormax, stood beside Elianora and said, "Elianora, we are so proud of you. You are kind, loving, and giving. Your mother will describe your amulet." He motioned with his red arms toward Verity.

Verity spoke up as she held out Elianora's amulet, saying, "Your amulet represents the tradition of tricolored dragons and their amulets. This amulet has three crystals melded together to form a flow in the shape of a beautiful flower. The flower shape is my special touch with the top starting with a teal crystal, blending into a sapphire-blue crystal, and then a marvelous purple crystal at the base. This represents your uniqueness and how special you really are to me and to every dragon. You have befriended and helped every dragon you have met. You have a special heart, and we love you."

Elianora hugged both her parents and took her place in line as her parents rejoined the clapping crowd.

Mr. Ferrix turned to the line of graduating dragons and said, "As you are now no longer dragonlings, you have been presented your amulets and are now acknowledged as graduated into being young adult dragons. Congratulations! We all look forward with anticipation to see how you will continue to grow in the future."

The crowd of dragons all clapped as the students stood proudly with their amulets shining around their necks.

As the dragons stood quietly, Mr. Ferrix said to them, "Next year, you will begin to learn how to be an adult dragon with your unique abilities and talents. Your new teachers eagerly await the coming year. I hope you are all excited to start your next adventure."

The young adult dragons all cheered and broke off to join their families. Elianora walked over to her mom and dad and asked, "Who was that old dragon I saw you talking with?"

Cormax patted Elianora on the back and answered, "He's an old friend. We've known him since before you hatched."

Elianora looked up at her father and asked, "Where did he go, and why did he leave?"

Verity responded, "He had somewhere he needed to be. I'm sure you'll get to meet him someday soon."

Elianora smiled as her parents began talking with the other parents around them. She thought, *I think there's more to that dragon than they are saying. Oh well, I'll leave that for another day. Today is a spectacular day with my friends and family. I'm going to enjoy it.*

About the Author

Conner Doyle is a high school graduate. He loved dragons from a very young age. He enjoys writing stories and creating worlds and characters. He loves dogs and cats. His favorite relaxation is to play video games. He often walks while thinking about characters and storylines. He cares about helping people and learning new things.